SEQUEL TO *WHEN HE HELD MY HAND*

JUSTICE
COURT OR KARMA?

A Gripping Tale of Resilience and Faith

DR. CRYSTAL

INDIA · SINGAPORE · MALAYSIA

ISBN
Paperback 979-8-89673-460-4
Hardcase 979-8-89699-405-3

Disclaimer

This book is a work of fiction.

Names, characters, businesses, places, events, locales,
and incidents are either the products of the author's
imagination or used in a fictitious manner.

Any resemblance to anyone living or dead, and real events
is purely coincidental.

Dedication

This book is dedicated to the memory of my late father, who left for the Heavenly Abode on 15th February 2020.

This book is also dedicated to the memory of my late mother, who left for the Heavenly Abode on 21st July 2009.

Contents

Acknowledgements

Writing this book has been an incredible journey, and I am deeply grateful to those who have supported and inspired me along the way.

Supreme Power

First and foremost, I express my heartfelt gratitude to the Supreme Power for guiding me through every step of life. Your presence has been a beacon of hope and strength, illuminating my path with wisdom and grace.

Legal Support

A special thanks to my esteemed lawyers in Mumbai and Surat. Your expertise and unwavering support have been invaluable in navigating the complexities and challenges that have come my way.

A Special Friend

To my special friend, who has always been a pillar of support throughout the ups and downs of my life. Your friendship is a cherished gift, and I am forever thankful for your constant encouragement and belief in me.

Friends and Well-Wishers

I am blessed to have a wonderful circle of friends, especially those from my school days, who have stood by me through thick and thin. Your camaraderie and laughter have been a source of joy and comfort, making this journey all the more meaningful. To all my well-wishers, your positive energy and good vibes have been a source of strength.

My Sons

Last but certainly not least, my deepest appreciation goes to my two wonderful sons, the apples of my eye. Your unwavering support and faith in every decision I have made have been my greatest motivation. You have stood by me through life's twists and turns, and for that, I am eternally grateful.

Thank you all for being a part of this incredible journey. Your love and support have made this book possible.

A New Perspective: Transforming Life's Journey

The journey of life is often compared to a long and winding road, an unpredictable path filled with both exhilarating highs and challenging lows. Along this road, we encounter moments of triumph and defeat, joy and sorrow. Each twist and turn brings its own set of obstacles, but also opportunities for growth and self-discovery. As we travel this road, the perspective we choose to adopt can significantly shape not only our experience but also our progress. The way we view the world around us and the challenges we face can either propel us forward or hold us back.

I vividly recall a story I once came across, a story that left an indelible mark on my soul. It was about Dr. Brahma Prakash, a mentor to the renowned scientist Dr. A.P.J. Abdul Kalam, who played a crucial role in shaping his outlook on life. Dr. Prakash's words of wisdom had such a profound effect on Kalam that they helped him navigate the complexities of life in his illustrious career. Those very same words, shared with me through a simple passage, resonated deeply within me, transforming my own way of thinking and my approach to life's challenges.

Dr. Prakash's words were simple, yet profoundly insightful:

"If you see this world as mean and rude, it will interfere with your concentration. Negative thinking is similar to carrying 20 bags of luggage on a trip. This baggage will make your trip miserable, and progress will be slow."

The Burden of Negativity

The metaphor of carrying 20 bags of luggage hit me like a wave. It was such a vivid and relatable comparison. Just as physical baggage can weigh us down, making our travels cumbersome and exhausting, emotional and mental baggage can similarly weigh us down on our journey through life. *Every negative thought, each lingering doubt, and every pessimistic belief adds an extra pound to our mental and emotional load.* These thoughts can cloud our vision, drain our energy, and prevent us from moving forward. In the same way that a heavy suitcase can slow down our travel, the weight of negativity can slow down our personal growth, productivity, and peace of mind.

This realization became an awakening for me. How many times had I carried unnecessary emotional weight—worries about the future, regrets from the past, and fears of failure? All of these burdens were slowing me down and preventing me from fully experiencing the richness of life. In fact, I had been so caught up in these negative thoughts that I hadn't realized the extent to which they were hindering my potential. The idea that negativity was like carrying multiple bags of heavy luggage was not just a clever metaphor; it was a truth I could feel deep within my own life.

Choosing a Different Path

Dr. Prakash's powerful insight opened my eyes to the fact that the key to overcoming the challenges of life lies not in changing the world around us, but in changing how we perceive it. *While we cannot always control the circumstances we find ourselves in, we do have control over our reactions, our mind-set, and our attitude.* By consciously deciding to see the world through a lens of positivity, curiosity, and possibility, we can lighten our emotional and mental load. This doesn't mean ignoring the difficulties that life throws at us or pretending that they don't exist. Rather, it means approaching those challenges with a mind-set that is open, hopeful, and solution-oriented.

Choosing positivity doesn't mean that we will never encounter hardship, but it means that we will face those hardships with resilience and strength. It is about seeing each obstacle as an opportunity for growth, every setback as a lesson, and every disappointment as a stepping stone toward something better. The power to change our experience begins with the choices we make in how we view the world around us.

The Power of Positive Thinking

Positive thinking, as Dr. Prakash suggests, is not merely about maintaining an upbeat attitude or pretending that everything is perfect when it's not. True positive thinking is about cultivating resilience in the face of adversity, enhance creativity in times of challenge, and opening ourselves up to the opportunities that await us, even when they seem hidden behind a veil of difficulty. It's about shifting our focus from what's wrong to what's possible.

When we let go of the unnecessary baggage of negativity— whether it's old grudges, fears of failure, or self-doubt—we free ourselves to embrace the present moment and the opportunities it offers. This shift in perspective creates space for new ideas, fresh experiences, and a deeper connection with our inner strength. *Positive thinking is not about denying reality; it's about embracing a mind-set that allows us to navigate life's realities with grace and confidence.*

Embracing a New Outlook

Since adopting this new perspective, inspired by Dr. Prakash's timeless wisdom, I have found a renewed sense of clarity and purpose in my life. *The world, as I now see it, is still filled with its fair share of challenges, obstacles, and hardships. Yet, my approach to these challenges has dramatically shifted. No longer do I view the world as mean and rude, a place full of unfair circumstances and injustices. Instead, I now see it as a place brimming with endless possibilities, opportunities for learning, and avenues for growth.*

In embracing a new way of thinking, I have discovered a sense of inner peace and optimism that I never knew was possible. The weight of negativity has lifted from my shoulders, and as a result, I can move forward with greater ease, enthusiasm, and joy. I am now more focused on what I can control—my thoughts, my actions, and my reactions—rather than fixating on external factors that are beyond my influence. By focusing on the positive aspects of life and letting go of the unnecessary burdens that once weighed me down, I find myself traveling a much lighter, more fulfilling path.

As I continue on this journey, I remain deeply grateful for the wisdom that has guided me toward this new perspective. It has opened my eyes to the beauty and potential of the world around me, reminding me that while we cannot control the challenges we face, we can always control the way we face them. **Life, after all, is not just about the road we travel—it's about how we travel it.**

This chapter in my life marks the beginning of a new way of thinking, one that I hope will inspire others to embark on their own journey of transformation. I encourage anyone reading this to reflect on the "***bags***" they are carrying and consider what it would feel like to let go of them. By lightening our load, we not only make the journey more enjoyable but also more meaningful. *So, let us choose to travel light, with a heart full of hope, and a mind open to the endless possibilities that lie ahead.*

Introduction

Reflections on the Present and the Journey Ahead

Date: 23rd April 2023

This early summer morning, as the first rays of sunlight filter through my window, I sit quietly with a steaming cup of Nescafe coffee, its robust aroma awakening both my senses and my thoughts. The world outside seems to hum with possibilities, yet my mind drifts inward, tracing the invisible threads of time—past, present, and future. I gaze absentmindedly at the ceiling, the patterns there mirroring the intricate labyrinth of my reflections. What lies ahead remains a mystery; after all, who among us can unravel the enigmatic designs of fate? The Universe, vast and timeless, guards these secrets, revealing them only in its own time.

Yet, amid this uncertainty, a quote by the historian Stephen Ambrose resonates deeply within me:

"The past is the source of knowledge, and the future is a source of hope. Love of the past implies faith in the future."

These words echo a comforting truth—that while the future may be unknowable, the lessons of yesterday and the promise of tomorrow can inspire unwavering hope today.

The Universal Law of Effort

Life, in its essence, is governed by a beautifully simple yet profoundly challenging law: the need for persistent effort. The Universe, impartial and unfailing, demands that we pour our hearts and minds into our endeavours with sincerity. The law doesn't cater to impatience; rewards do not arrive hastily or undeservedly. Instead, they manifest when the timing is right—when our efforts align harmoniously with the rhythm of the cosmos.

This understanding compels me to act, not with the expectation of immediate gratification, but with faith in the ultimate fairness of life's processes. *Hard work, when genuine and relentless, bears fruit in ways we may not always foresee but can always trust.*

A Journey Interrupted Yet Continued

If these words find you, it means you've already walked alongside me through the pages of my first book, **"When He Held My Hand"**, a story that unfolded during the unprecedented chaos of the COVID-19 pandemic. The narrative paused abruptly, just as I was preparing to take a decisive legal step against Dolion and Batibat in late March 2020. But then the world stopped.

India's nationwide lockdown in mid-March 2020 froze not just daily life but the wheels of justice themselves. Courtrooms fell silent, their halls devoid of the usual fervour. It wasn't until late 2021 that proceedings resumed, and with them, my hope for resolution. However, fate had yet another twist in store. In May 2022, on the cusp of a judgment, the presiding judge was transferred, and the case once again fell into limbo.

Justice, it seems, is a patient game, but so am I.

The Strength of Perseverance

Through these trials, I have learned an invaluable lesson: perseverance is not merely a virtue but a way of life. The obstacles I face do not weaken my resolve; they fortify it. I have faith that my unwavering commitment will eventually light the path to success. Perhaps the journey has not yet yielded results because I still have more to give, more to learn, and more to grow.

Failure, I now realize, is not an endpoint but a necessary stepping stone. It is a teacher, guiding me toward greater resilience and understanding. The words of Colin Powell inspire me in moments of doubt:

"There are no secrets to success. It is the result of preparation, hard work, and learning from failure."

The Gift of Now

As I pen these thoughts, I am struck by the profound simplicity of a timeless truth:

"Yesterday is History, Tomorrow is a Mystery, Today is a Gift of God, which is why we call it The Present."

This mantra reminds me to live in the moment, to appreciate the here and now as a sacred gift. It urges me to savour the journey, regardless of its pace or destination, and to find joy even in the small victories along the way.

Life is a tapestry woven with threads of challenges, triumphs, and lessons. Each day adds a new strand, enriching the pattern. As I move forward, my heart brims with gratitude for the experiences that have shaped me, the hope that propels me, and the faith that sustains me.

The journey continues, and I am ready to embrace it all.

Chapter 1

Unearthing Hidden Talents

A Journey of Rediscovery

As the world came to a standstill during the Covid lockdown in March 2020, life in India took on a meditative stillness. With bustling streets transformed into silent lanes and vibrant routines replaced by introspection, the air was thick with both uncertainty and opportunity. It was a period unlike any other—a chance to step back, reflect, and reconnect with parts of ourselves long overlooked.

Eudora Welty's words resonated deeply: *"The events in our lives happen in a sequence in time, but in their significance to ourselves they find their own order, a timetable not necessarily—perhaps not possibly—chronological."*

For me, this unexpected pause became a canvas where hidden talents, buried under years of monotony, came alive with renewed vigour.

Discovering a New Passion

Confined to my home, I sought refuge in a space I had often overlooked—the kitchen. This space, which had previously served as little more than a functional corner, transformed into a sanctuary of creativity and experimentation. Amid the clinking of utensils and the gentle hum of the oven, I found myself drawn to the art of baking. What began as a humble attempt to pass the time blossomed into a full-fledged passion.

Alongside my demanding responsibilities as an online consulting doctor, I began experimenting with recipes, focusing on creating healthy yet delicious treats. Muffins quickly became my specialty—a perfect blend of wholesome nutrition and indulgent flavours. My kitchen turned into a laboratory of sorts, where I honed my craft, perfecting recipes that balanced taste and health. Each batch represented more than food; it was a tangible reminder of growth and discovery.

Word spread among friends and neighbours, and soon I found myself baking muffins not just for personal joy but for eager customers. The aroma of freshly baked goods often filled my home in the early hours of the morning as I worked tirelessly to fulfil orders. *My promise was simple yet heartfelt: every muffin would be homemade, healthy, and delivered fresh on the same day.* The satisfaction of seeing my creations brighten someone's day made every late night and early morning worth the effort.

A Taste of Success

Encouraged by the growing demand and positive feedback, I took a bold step—I entered online competitions centered around healthy baking. To my amazement, I won several of these contests. The accolades were not just symbols of success; they were beacons of hope in an otherwise challenging time. *Each win served as a reminder that even amid uncertainty, the human spirit could find ways to thrive and shine.*

These small victories provided much-needed motivation as I balanced baking with my professional duties and prepared for future legal battles awaiting the reopening of courts. They reminded me that personal growth and fulfilment often emerge in the most unexpected circumstances.

Inspiring Others to Shine

My journey of self-discovery soon extended beyond myself. I felt an urge to inspire others to explore their own hidden talents. One friend, Kamla, a classmate from school now residing in Bangalore, came to mind. She often confided in me about feeling a sense of unfulfillment, despite her children being well-settled in Dubai. During one conversation, I recalled her fondly speaking about a prize she had won for her Hyderabadi Biryani while in Dubai.

Seizing this as an opportunity, I encouraged her to revisit her passion for cooking. With a little nudging, she began taking small steps, and before long, her talent transformed into a thriving home-based business. Today, she is inundated with orders for her signature biryani, cutlets, and other culinary delights. Watching her rediscover her purpose and build something meaningful filled me with an indescribable joy. It reinforced the idea that sometimes, *all it takes is a gentle push to set someone on a path of self-discovery.*

A Lesson in Compassion

This chapter of my life taught me something profound: *our connection to the Supreme Power is mirrored in how we treat those around us.* Every small act of kindness, encouragement, or support holds the potential to ripple outwards, touching lives in ways we may never fully grasp.

In a time of global crisis, the rediscovery of hidden talents became more than a personal triumph; it became a way to connect, inspire, and uplift. Whether it's finding solace in baking, rekindling an old passion, or simply listening with genuine interest, we all have the power to make a difference. Let us carry this lesson forward, nurturing the seeds of creativity and compassion within ourselves and those around us. After all, *the beauty of life lies not just in what we achieve but in how we inspire others to unearth the treasures within their own hearts.*

Chapter 2

Transforming Time into a Tool for Justice

"The key is not spending time but in investing it."
– Stephen R. Covey

Days flowed into weeks, and weeks blended seamlessly into months. The fleeting nature of time often bewilders the human mind, giving the impression that it hastens when we least expect it. In truth, *time is a constant force, neither speeding up nor slowing down, merely marching forward at its unwavering pace.* Yet, its perception bends to our experiences. When immersed in joy or engaged in meaningful pursuits, we often find ourselves marvelling at how quickly the hours fade away.

But what of time spent in struggle? In those moments, its passage can feel unbearably slow, like trudging through an endless desert, searching for an oasis that seems always out of reach.

The Struggle for Justice

I found myself engulfed in such a desert, fighting a battle that felt eternal. My quest for justice for my father had become an exhausting marathon, with no clear finish line in sight. Each day brought new doubts, gnawing at my resolve. *Would I ever see the scales of justice tip in my favour? Was I chasing a dream destined to remain unfulfilled?*

Dolion, the architect of my suffering, seemed invincible. He navigated the loopholes of the legal system with a devilish precision, slipping through cracks like water escaping a clenched fist. His wealth, amassed through deceit and corruption, fortified him against accountability. Each victory he claimed was a bitter reminder of the uphill battle I faced.

But I could not afford the luxury of despair. Time, I realized, was a resource I could no longer squander. Instead of letting it slip through my fingers, I resolved to wield it like a weapon. I began dissecting every detail of my case with renewed determination. *Was there something I had missed? A path unexplored? A stone unturned?*

I refused to let the enormity of the task paralyze me. Every visit to the courthouse, every sleepless night poring over documents, every conversation with my lawyer became an investment in the justice I sought. *The journey was gruelling, but I pressed on, fuelled by the memory of my father and the unwavering belief that his dignity deserved to be restored.*

Realization and Resolve

After countless nights of introspection, the fog of doubt began to lift. My struggle wasn't born of laziness or incompetence; it was the result of facing an adversary who thrived on manipulation and greed. Dolion had not only stolen my rightful share but had weaponized his ill-gotten wealth to bend the system to his will. *Bribery, coercion, and deception were his tools, and with them, he strutted through life with an arrogance that made my blood boil.*

But arrogance is a fragile shield, one that cracks under the weight of truth. I reminded myself that justice, though slow, has a habit of catching up to even the most cunning of foes. My faith, unwavering and steadfast, became my anchor. I believed in the **Divine Balance of the Universe— that a Higher Power would ultimately guide the truth into the light.**

"Time is the wisest of all things that are, for it brings everything to you." Thales

Time, I knew, was both my greatest ally and my sternest teacher. It demanded patience and perseverance, testing my spirit at every turn. Yet, it also offered wisdom, clarity, and the promise of eventual resolution. I held onto that promise with all my might, determined to see this journey through to its end.

I am confident that, in time, the truth will prevail, and justice will be served. My journey may be arduous, but I am resolute in my pursuit. *Time, with its intrinsic wisdom, will bring the scales of justice into balance.*

Chapter 3

Dolion's Expertise: Knowledge as a Double - Edged Sword

The Shadows of Truth: A journey of Scepticism

"A thing is not proved just because no one has ever questioned it. What has never been gone into impartially has never been properly gone into. Hence, scepticism is the first step towards truth. It must be applied generally, because it is the touchstone." — Denis Diderot

A Calm Examination: Uncovering Deception

With a cool mind, I scrutinized the situation at hand. Being a doctor, Dolion was well aware of the critical dangers associated with improper use of insulin. ***For a non-diabetic, the administration of insulin or antidiabetic medicines could result in catastrophic consequences if left untreated for a mere 4-5 hours. The outcome could be as severe as brain death or even fatality.***

My father suffered such a tragic fate. On the 29th of September 2019, he was administered insulin or antidiabetic medicines by Dolion and Batibat. This led to him being in a state of brain death for four and a half months. Ultimately, he departed from this world on the 15th of February 2020.

Medical Insights: Insulin Misuse: The Silent Weapon

Just to share a crucial medical fact—insulin administered to non-diabetics can lead to a hypoglycaemic coma. This condition results in a loss of consciousness, severe and irreversible brain injuries, or potentially death.

Dolion, being a doctor, was acutely aware of the pharmacokinetics of insulin. When injected into subcutaneous tissue, insulin monomers and dimers are swiftly absorbed by blood capillaries. *Given insulin's short half-life in the body, detecting insulin abuse through laboratory tests becomes exceedingly challenging.*

The Complex Web: Deception cloaked in Expertise

In addition to his medical practice, Dolion also worked for several pharmaceutical companies. This dual role granted him insight into the less conventional uses of insulin—**A GRAND DAME with HIDDEN ACES,** as one might say. These non-diabetic applications of insulin are not widely known, yet Dolion's knowledge in this area was extensive.

As I delved deeper into the shadows of this truth, I realized that scepticism was indeed the first step towards unveiling the reality hidden beneath layers of deception. *The time had come to question everything that had been left unquestioned for too long.*

Chapter 4

The Genesis of Betrayal and The Master Plan

"Planning is bringing the future into the present so that you can do something about it now."
— *Alan Lakein*

Dolion's Strategic Blueprint of Control

Every great endeavour begins with a plan. Not just any plan, but one that is deliberate, strategic, and crafted with precision. In the following chapters, we will journey into the depths of the **Master Plan—*a meticulous, almost sinister blueprint designed by the Master Mind.*** But before we dissect its intricacies and unveil its layers, we must pause and reflect on the very heart of any undertaking: Understanding the **Why?**

The "Why?" Behind The Web of Deceit

To understand the plan, one must understand the driving force behind it. It all began with an act of betrayal so profound that it fractured the foundation of trust within our family.

Dolion, a man whose actions were as cold as they were calculated, had stripped my parents of everything they owned. Through a chilling blend of coercion, deceit, and forgery, he seized their ancestral properties, shares, jewellery, and cash. My parents, once proud and self-reliant, were reduced to nothing more than shadows of their former selves, left with little more than the clothes on their backs. *In Dolion's eyes, they were no longer people—they were burdens, relics to be ignored, as insignificant as the furniture in the home they had once cherished.*

But Dolion's ambitions didn't stop there. Together with Batibat, his equally conniving accomplice, they dreamed of a life abroad, far from the remnants of the family they had destroyed. With two of their children comfortably settled in Australia, they envisioned a perfect escape—one filled with the laughter of grandchildren and the freedom to live unencumbered. Yet, **one obstacle stood in their way: my elderly parents.**

I had made my intentions clear. Through family channels, I expressed my willingness, even eagerness, to care for my parents. I wanted to offer them the peace and respect they deserved after a lifetime of hardships. But Dolion, consumed by his own guilt and paranoia, refused to believe in the sincerity of my intentions. In his warped, narcissistic worldview, he assumed I would behave as he had—driven by greed and selfishness. He feared that if my parents came to live with me, I would demand my rightful share of the inheritance he had stolen.

For a man like Dolion, the thought of relinquishing even an inch of his ill-gotten power was intolerable. Narcissism fuelled his every move, and his need to maintain control outweighed any moral consideration. To secure his grip on the family's assets and dictate the future, he devised *The Strategic Plan*—a carefully orchestrated scheme that would ensure his dominance while isolating my parents from any potential allies.

The Start of Something Monumental

This plan, rooted in cunning and manipulation, marked the beginning of a chain of events that would forever alter the trajectory of our lives. It wasn't just a plan—***it was a masterstroke of strategy, a chilling reminder of how far some will go to protect their illusions of power and control.***

As we peel back the layers of this Master Plan, you will come to see the depths of its treachery. You will learn the motives that drove it, the methods that enabled it, and the devastating consequences it left in its wake. *This story is not merely about a plan—it is about resilience, justice, and the enduring fight to reclaim what was lost.*

Chapter 5

A Mother's Silent Suffering

"Mom, sometimes I wish you could come back, but I don't want you to suffer again. I know you are with me, and I will always love and miss you with all my heart. Until we meet again."

These words echoed in my mind as I recalled the painful memories of my mother's struggles. Her once vibrant spirit was slowly dimmed by an unrelenting backache that seemed to have taken control of her life. It was heart-wrenching to witness her suffering, especially knowing that much of it could have been alleviated with proper care.

The Unheeded Cry for Help

My mother's ordeal began with a persistent backache. However, as the pain intensified, it became clear that something more serious was at play. Yet, *the only solution offered by Dolion, her primary caregiver, was a steady stream of painkillers.*

I remember the phone calls vividly, her voice tinged with frustration and despair. *"All he gives me are painkillers,"* she would say. *"They're not helping, and now my stomach is on fire from all the acidity they cause."*

Despite her obvious discomfort and the side effects from the medication, Dolion seemed indifferent to her pleas for a more comprehensive examination. *His deaf ear to her suffering only compounded her sense of helplessness.*

The Offer of Sanctuary

Desperate to provide her with some relief, I suggested that she come stay with me. I could arrange for her to see an orthopaedic specialist, someone who could properly diagnose and treat her condition. But my offer was met with palpable fear.

She was terrified of Dolion and his partner, Batibat. The mere thought of leaving their care, even for a brief period, filled her with dread. *"What if they find out?"* she whispered, her voice quivering with anxiety. *"I can't risk it… I just can't."*

Her fear was a barrier too high to cross, and I was left feeling helpless, unable to rescue my own mother from her silent torment.

One day, amidst the whirlwind of emotions and pain, my mother found herself confiding in her dearest friend, Aunt Lydia. Aunt Lydia, always a beacon of support and understanding, was taken aback by the revelation of my mother's suffering. Without a moment's hesitation, she marched straight to Dolion's room, confronting him with a stern ultimatum. If he could not ensure my mother received the necessary medical attention, Aunt Lydia would arrange for her son, Joe, to step in. Dolion, with his narcissistic tendencies, was more concerned about his reputation than anything else. To save face, he hurriedly took my mother to Lilaben Hospital.

The Dilemma

At the hospital, the orthopaedic surgeon delivered a grave assessment: *"You were late in coming for treatment. Now it will be a high-risk surgery."* This pronouncement posed a significant dilemma. Dolion, being a covert narcissist, immediately set his network of enablers, often referred to as **"flying monkeys,"** into motion to protect his image.

One of these enablers, Myna, a relative, reached out to me. She inquired about the course of action regarding my mother's surgery. I was acutely aware of the manipulative game Dolion was orchestrating. The surgeon's warning labelled the surgery as high-risk. If I consented to the surgery, my mother could potentially die during or after the procedure. On the other hand, if I refused, her back pain would persist, and Dolion would easily shift the blame onto me, ensuring that he remained untouched by any fault or consequence.

Standing My Ground

I maintained my composure and asked Myna why my opinion suddenly held weight. She responded by emphasizing my role as the daughter of the house. Without hesitation, I candidly expressed to her that my involvement as a daughter seemed to be conveniently recognized only when it suited Dolion's whims. I questioned the absence of my other legal rights as a daughter. Moreover, I instructed Myna to relay to Dolion that I was fully aware of his manipulative tactics. I told her that he was free to make any decision he deemed fit, but *he must bear the responsibility for the consequences of neglecting timely treatment for my mother.*

In my heart, I knew with certainty that I was doing the right thing. It was imperative to stand firm, unyielding in the face of manipulation and deceit.

I am sure, (Dolion, himself, had admitted to a close friend) that his delay in treating my mother had contributed to her demise. This truth will always weigh heavily on my heart and mind.

A Day of Rain and Resilience

The day of the surgery arrived with torrential rain, as if the heavens were mirroring my inner turmoil. Streets and railway lines were flooded, but I was determined to reach the hospital. Navigating through the chaos, I finally arrived just in time to see my mother being wheeled into the operation theatre. *It felt like a final goodbye.* I embraced her, tears streaming down my face. I could sense her desire to confide in me. Yet, Batibat, ever vigilant, refused to leave us alone. She feared my mother would reveal the mistreatment she endured from her son and daughter-in-law, and that I would use this information against them.

Lost Moments and Lingering Regret

To this day, I regret losing those precious last moments with my mother. Anger and resentment towards Batibat linger, knowing that those moments can never be reclaimed. The surgery itself was successful, but my mother faced complications afterward. Placed on a ventilator, she regained consciousness for a brief moment two days later. My cousin sister was present at the time, and my mother, with her last ounce of strength, requested a piece of paper. She wrote my name on it before slipping back into unconsciousness. It was a testament to her love and the bond we shared, a bond that transcended the chaos around us.

Two days later, on the 21st of July 2009, my mother passed away. Her departure left a void in my life, filled with unresolved emotions and questions. *Even today, I hold onto that piece of paper with my name on it, a cherished reminder of her final thoughts of me.*

I hold Dolion solely responsible for pushing my mother towards her untimely death, which he himself admitted later to his friend.

Chapter 6

A Father's Echo

"No matter how old we are, we still need our dads and wonder how we'll get by without them." - Jennifer Williamson

The Remarkable Man Behind the Legacy

My father was a remarkable man, an extraordinary blend of strength and wisdom. Even as the relentless grip of senile dementia clouded his later years, his physical health remained a marvel. *He was neither diabetic nor hypertensive, and his heart, both literally and metaphorically, was strong and unwavering.* It was a rare blessing to witness a man whose body seemed almost untouched by time, even as his mind wandered into the misty recesses of memory.

The Loneliness of a Strong Man

Yet, despite his physical robustness, there was an unmistakable vulnerability in his eyes whenever I visited him. *It wasn't the vulnerability of age or illness but of a man grappling with loneliness and fear.* Living alone, with my brother Dolion and his wife Batibat constantly globe-trotting, left him anxious and adrift. ***He often lamented how the simplest needs—like a meal at the right time—were left unmet.*** His words would trail off into sighs, his hands trembling ever so slightly as he expressed his longing for a sense of security and connection.

A Plea for Fairness and a Reminder of Rights

"Stay here," he would plead, his voice a mixture of desperation and hope. *"This house is your home too. One of these two flats is rightfully yours."* His insistence came from a desire to restore fairness, to reclaim what was his—and, by extension, mine. When I reminded him that Dolion and Batibat had taken over both flats, properties that belonged to him and my late mother, he would shake his head in dismay. *"They've done it illegally,"* he'd assert, his voice firm despite the frailty of his body. ***"Fight for your rights. Remember, God is watching. And so am I. Even after I'm gone, I'll make sure you get what's rightfully yours."***

Now, as I sit here in April 2023, three long years since his passing, his words resonate more strongly than ever. For the first time in this arduous journey, I see a flicker of light—a glimmer of hope in my quest for justice. The path has been long and fraught with obstacles, but I feel an unseen force propelling me forward. It is as if my father's blessings, coupled with the grace of the Supreme Power, are guiding my every step.

The Lawyer's Voice: An Otherworldly Connection

And then, there is my lawyer in Surat. This man, a stranger until recently, possesses something extraordinary: his voice. *It is uncanny, almost otherworldly, how much it resembles my father's.* Every time he speaks, it sends a chill down my spine. It's not just a resemblance; *it feels like my father himself, speaking to me through this man.* His tone, his cadence, the gentle yet resolute way he delivers his words—***it's as though my father has returned from the heavens to stand by me in this fight.***

> *"No, I never saw an Angel, but it is irrelevant whether*
> *I saw one or not. I feel their presence around me."*
> —Paulo Coelho

I cannot explain it, but I no longer feel alone. I feel my father's presence in ways that defy logic. It's as if he's right here, championing my cause with the same passion and determination he had in the last few months of his life. His voice, carried through the lawyer, reminds me that the bonds of love, justice, and family do not end with death. They transcend time, space, and even the boundaries of life itself.

This realization has brought me immense comfort and strength. My father may no longer walk this earth, but his spirit lives on—in my heart, in the guidance of the divine, and, most hauntingly, in the voice of the lawyer who now fights by my side. *It's as if the Universe itself has conspired to remind me that Justice, though delayed, is never beyond reach.* My father's echo reverberates through every step of this journey, a powerful testament to the enduring force of love and the unyielding pursuit of what is right.

Chapter 7

The Unchanging Nature of Narcissism

Understanding human behaviour is often like navigating an intricate maze—there are twists, turns, and dead ends that make it challenging to predict how people will act. This is especially true when dealing with individuals who seem impervious to personal growth or self-reflection. *Some people never acknowledge their flaws, let alone admit to their wrongdoings.* They sidestep accountability, resist self-improvement, and, most tellingly, rarely—if ever— offer a sincere apology. These patterns are not random; they are defining traits of a deeper issue. This was the case with Dolion and Batibat, whose actions after the incident involving my mother perfectly encapsulated the static, unchanging nature of narcissism.

You might think that after such an emotionally charged event, they would have been motivated to extend kindness or care to my father, recognizing the gravity of their past mistakes. However, ***Dolion—a master of covert manipulation***—had different plans. *His focus wasn't on* *healing wounds or making amends; it was on advancing his own self-serving agenda, no matter the cost to others.*

Traits of a Narcissist

If there's one thing to know about narcissists, it's that their behaviour is defined by patterns. Understanding these patterns is key to making sense of their actions. Below are three defining traits that narcissists exhibit time and again:

1) *They Never Express Genuine Remorse*

   Narcissists are incapable of feeling true regret for the pain or harm they inflict on others. Apologies, when they do offer them, are insincere and often serve as tools for manipulation rather than heartfelt expressions of empathy.

2) *They Refuse to Take Responsibility*

   A narcissist will go to great lengths to avoid accountability. Whether it's shifting blame, denying their actions, or outright lying, they craft elaborate narratives to absolve themselves of any wrongdoing.

3) *They Prioritize Achieving Over Earning*

   For narcissists, the journey is irrelevant—it's all about the destination. They crave success, recognition, and status but are rarely willing to put in the effort or personal growth needed to earn those rewards. Their focus is on shortcuts, manipulations, and appearances rather than authentic accomplishment.

The Role of Materialism in Narcissism

Narcissists are driven by external validation. For them, *wealth, possessions, and social status are not just desirable—they are essential tools in crafting the image they wish to project.* Dolion exemplified this obsession perfectly. *Long before my father's health became a concern, he had already taken control of everything my parents and grandparents had worked to build.* To someone like Dolion, possessions weren't just things—*they were trophies that validated his importance and elevated his standing in the eyes of others.*

This fixation on materialism often leads to financial exploitation within relationships. It's not enough for a narcissist to have what they need—they must have more, and they must have it at the expense of others. The possessions, the status, the image—they all serve as armour to shield their fragile egos from the harsh reality of their emotional emptiness.

The Strategic Façade

For narcissists like Dolion, life is a performance, and the world is their stage. They meticulously craft their image to command admiration, masking the void where genuine connection and empathy should reside. *Everything they do is calculated, from their charm in public to their cruelty in private.* Dolion's treatment of my father wasn't driven by care or concern; it was dictated by what served his narrative and bolstered his reputation.

Understanding these traits illuminates the inner workings of individuals like Dolion. It's not about what they feel—they rarely allow themselves to feel anything deeply. *It's about what they want: power, admiration, and control. In the end, their actions reveal a truth they can never admit—that their carefully curated image is as hollow as the empathy they refuse to show.*

By recognizing these patterns, we can better understand the motives behind their actions, protect ourselves from their manipulation, and, most importantly, learn to prioritize relationships built on authenticity and respect rather than appearances.

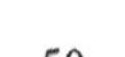

Chapter 8

The Master Plan

A Dream of Togetherness

Dolion and Batibat stood on the cusp of realizing a dream they had nurtured for years—a dream that promised not just a change of scenery, but a chance to live out their golden years surrounded by the love and laughter of family. Their children had long since settled in Australia, carving out successful lives of their own, and the couple yearned to join them, to bask in the warmth of their grandchildren's hugs and watch them grow up first-hand. It was a vision that filled their hearts with hope, and as the years weighed heavier on their shoulders, this vision became a necessity.

The Obstacles In The Way

There was nothing unnatural or wrong about wanting to spend one's later years close to family. After all, who wouldn't want to embrace the joy of togetherness in the twilight of life? But life, as it so often does, had placed a formidable obstacle in their way—one that would require more than mere longing to overcome.

My father, a man of remarkable resilience and health, was now in his 90s and still going strong. His presence in our lives was a testament to the vitality of the human spirit. However, he had inadvertently become the centre of a quiet yet significant storm. Dolion, ever the planner, had no intention of relinquishing my father to my care. For Dolion, my father was not just a familial responsibility but a piece in a larger puzzle—a puzzle that would soon reveal itself in the unfolding of their "master plan."

The Master Plan Unfolds: A Bold Step Forward

Early in September 2019, Dolion and Batibat boarded a flight to Australia, hearts brimming with excitement and minds alive with possibilities. This trip wasn't just another visit to see their children; it was reconnaissance. During their stay, Dolion stumbled upon a property—a stunning, luxurious apartment in the very neighbourhood where his son lived. It was modern, spacious, and everything they could have hoped for in their dream home. The decision was made almost immediately: they would buy it and make Australia their permanent home.

The Financial Puzzle

But dreams, especially those involving migration and real estate, don't come cheap. Dolion, a man known for his meticulous calculations, began to piece together the financial puzzle. He had already initiated the paperwork for migration, and now he turned his attention to the funds needed for this ambitious move.

This is where things took a darker turn. Dolion's plan hinged on selling two valuable flats in the Swaraj Cooperative Housing Society in Vile Parle—flats that, by rights, belonged to my parents. One of these homes had been a cherished gift from my maternal grandparents to my mother upon her marriage, a symbol of love and support. The other flat had been purchased by my father through years of hard work and savings. *These homes were more than bricks and mortar; they were a testament to my parents' journey, their legacy.*

The Audacious Move

Yet, through a series of cunning and calculated moves, Dolion and Batibat had managed to have their names inscribed on the share certificates of both flats. It was a manoeuvre that had stunned me, not just for its audacity but for the cold disregard it showed for what these properties truly represented.

And so, as I write this chapter, I find myself embroiled in a legal battle—a fight for justice, a fight for what is right. The case, filed with the registrar, is far from resolved. The uncertainty looms large, but my resolve remains unshaken. *This isn't just about property; it's about preserving the truth, honouring my parents' legacy, and standing up against a plan that sought to erase all of that for personal gain.*

For Dolion and Batibat, this was a calculated move, a critical step in their master plan. ***For me, it was a call to arms, a reminder that sometimes, in the face of injustice, we have no choice but to rise and fight.***

Chapter 9

A Turn Towards Justice

Finding Peace In Simplicity

Until 2019, I had carefully refrained from taking any legal action against Dolion and Batibat. It wasn't because I lacked opportunities or the will to fight but because my heart was at peace. The Universe had blessed me in ways that truly mattered. I found joy and contentment in the simple yet profound gifts of life. My basic needs—food, shelter, and clothing—were met without struggle. Beyond that, I was surrounded by love and warmth: a supportive family, loyal friends, and the intangible but essential threads of compassion and affection. *With these riches in my life, I felt calm, balanced, and fulfilled.*

Reflections on Past Struggles

My first book, "***When He Held My Hand***", offered readers an intimate look into the struggles that had shaped me, weaving together a tapestry of hardship, resilience, and hope. Within those pages, I candidly recounted the pain and injustice I had endured at the hands of Dolion and

Batibat. Their treatment of me had been cruel, but I had always been a firm believer in the *Natural Law of Karma.* I trusted that those who acted with malice and selfish intent would, in time, find their actions mirrored back at them in ways they could not escape.

For years, I chose to let the Universe take the reins, trusting that Divine Justice would prevail. Dolion and Batibat's behaviour had not gone unnoticed by me, but I didn't allow their negativity to poison my heart. I convinced myself that they would eventually reap what they had sown and that their brokenness would be their burden to bear, not mine.

The Catalyst: A Line Crossed

But then, something shifted. *My resolve to stand back and let the Universe work was shattered when their cruelty extended beyond me—to my parents.* **Their heartless actions led to the untimely and tragic deaths of two people I loved more than life itself.** This was no longer just about me. Their betrayal had crossed a line I could never forgive.

In those dark moments, the words of Benjamin Franklin echoed in my mind: *"Justice will not be served until those who are unaffected are as outraged as those who are."* I realized that justice wasn't just an abstract ideal; it was a responsibility.

A Decision to Claim Justice

For years, I had told myself that I didn't need to claim my rightful share of the property. *Material possessions had never been my priority.* I believed that Dolion and Batibat would, one day, have to answer to a higher power for their selfishness and cruelty. *I thought that letting go was an act of strength, a way to rise above their pettiness.*

But life, as it often does, had other plans for me. ***The turning point came on a day that will forever be etched in my memory: September 29, 2019***. On that fateful day, Dolion and Batibat committed an unforgivable act of cruelty. They administered insulin or antidiabetic medications to my father in a calculated manner, leaving him brain-dead and robbing him of the dignity he deserved. ***It was an act of cold-blooded malice that tore through my soul and left me with no choice but to act.***

This was no longer about property or pride. It was about standing up for the people I loved, the values I held dear, and the justice that my parents deserved. The Universe, it seemed, had been quietly nudging me toward this path all along, sending signs that I could no longer ignore.

A New Chapter Begins

With a heart heavy with grief but resolute with purpose, I decided to fight back. *This was not just about reclaiming what was rightfully mine; it was about honouring the memory of my parents and holding Dolion and Batibat accountable for their actions.*

This marked the beginning of a new chapter in my life—a chapter defined by courage, justice, and healing. I knew the road ahead would not be easy, but I also knew that I was no longer alone. The same Universe that had blessed me with love, compassion, and resilience would guide me on this journey toward justice.

And so, I stepped forward, ready to write the next pages of my story. *This time, I was not just the protagonist of my life but also its defender—a warrior for truth, justice, and the memory of those I had lost.*

Chapter 10

Synchronicity and Divine Guidance

The Divine Tapestry of Life

As I sit in quiet reflection, contemplating the intricate threads woven into the tapestry of life, I am struck by the awe-inspiring beauty of Divine Timing. It is nothing short of miraculous how the Universe—or perhaps God in His infinite wisdom—seems to orchestrate the encounters, moments, and events that ultimately shape our journeys. Like the Master Conductor of a grand symphony, God places the right people—friends, family, acquaintances, and even strangers—into our lives precisely when we need them most. Sometimes, these moments seem so perfectly aligned that they leave us no choice but to pause, marvel, and whisper, ***"This couldn't just be a coincidence."***

This realization has been one of my life's most profound lessons: ***everything happens for a reason***. Whether we can see it immediately or only in hindsight, there is a Divine Plan at work. And just as these people are placed on our paths, we, too, find ourselves positioned exactly where we are meant to be at just the right moment, ready to play our part in someone else's story.

Understanding Synchronicities

Synchronicities are so much more than random happenings or chance occurrences. They are like Divine breadcrumbs, thoughtfully scattered along the path of life to guide us toward something greater. They speak to us in whispers and nudges, pointing us toward the answers we seek, the lessons we need to learn, or the opportunities we might otherwise overlook.

Often dismissed as mere coincidence, synchronicities are, in truth, profound messages sent by our Angels, Spiritual Guides, the Universe, or God Himself. They are the language of the Divine, crafted to awaken us to possibilities we hadn't yet considered. These moments carry an energy that feels simultaneously mysterious and deeply familiar, as though the Universe itself is saying, ***"Pay attention. This is important."***

I often think of the words of intuitive expert Robert Ohotto, who describes synchronicity as *"a powerful force that moves through all our lives, offering intuitive guidance, needed wake-up calls, signs, new opportunities, revelations of one's life purpose, open doors, and access to new unlived potential."* The trick, of course, is recognizing these signs when they appear—and then having the courage to act on them, even when doing so defies logic or reason.

Signs of Synchronicity In My Life

The First Sign

Why was I, of all places, in the same building in Aunt Lydia's house on the very day my father was rushed to the hospital? His blood sugar level had plummeted to a critically low 18 mg/dL—a medical emergency that could have taken his life in minutes. At that moment, I couldn't help but feel the presence of Divine Intervention. If God hadn't wanted me to discover the truth behind my father's untimely passing, would He have placed me there, at that precise time? This wasn't just a coincidence. It was a call to action—a Divine Nudge urging me to look deeper and seek answers.

The Second Sign

Later that same day, as I was preparing to leave Aunt Lydia's house and head back to my residence in Borivali, the watchman arrived with urgent news. My father's condition had taken a dire turn. Had the watchman not appeared at that exact moment, the message could have been delayed or distorted. I shudder to think how *Dolion and Batibat—* individuals I now recognize as *covert manipulators—might have used the delay to alter hospital records or conceal the truth.* This synchronicity was a shield against deceit, a reminder of the Divine Timing that protects us even when we are unaware of it.

Dolion's history of manipulation was not new to me. I had written about it in my earlier book, "***When He Held***

My Hand", where I recounted similar schemes during my uncle's passing. And yet, in this moment, I felt a sense of clarity and purpose, as though God was saying, **"This time, you will not be deceived."**

Embracing Divine Guidance

My father departed for his Heavenly Abode on February 15, 2020—a date etched into my heart forever. That day, amid the pain and grief, I felt a quiet peace. I clung to the belief that God has a plan for each of us, even when we cannot fully understand it. My prayer was simple but earnest: *"Lord, give me the wisdom to recognize Your signs, the patience to trust Your timing, and the courage to follow wherever You lead."*

Reflecting on these synchronicities has taught me to remain open to the Divine Guidance that surrounds us. It's easy to dismiss these moments as random or coincidental, but when we do, we risk missing the profound truths they carry. They remind us that we are not alone, that there is a Higher Order at work, and that we are all part of something far greater than ourselves.

So, let us pay attention. Let us trust the whispers of the Universe and follow the signs it so lovingly places in our path. For when we do, we unlock the door to our greatest potential and step fully into the life we were always meant to live.

Chapter 11

A Relentless Pursuit of Justice

More than four years have passed, and yet, my resolve remains unshaken. My life has transformed into an intricate maze of legal battles, each turn marked by challenges, resilience, and an unwavering pursuit of truth. *Among the many struggles I face, one stands out as the most personal and profound—the fight for justice for my father.* It is a journey riddled with obstacles, not least because the judiciary, for all its virtues, operates on the foundation of tangible evidence.

The Challenge of Lost Evidence

From the very beginning, my path was deliberately obstructed. My brother, with calculated malice, orchestrated the disappearance of critical evidence. When my father was admitted to the hospital, no proper medical history was recorded. This was no mere oversight but a deliberate act, facilitated by the consulting doctor—a close confidant of my brother. *Vital procedures that could have uncovered the truth were conveniently ignored.*

No Medico Legal Complaint (MLC) was filed at the time of admission, an omission that would prove to be devastating. Tests that could have been game-changers, like analysing stomach contents or conducting a C-Peptide test in blood and urine, were never performed. These tests would have revealed alarmingly high insulin levels in my father's system, proving without a doubt that my non-diabetic father had been administered insulin or anti-diabetic medication. This sinister act caused his blood sugar to plummet to a life-threatening 18 mg/dL.

The Unrelenting Hurdles of Corruption

Days later, after relentless pressure on my part, an MLC was finally filed. But it came too late—four days too late. By then, vital clues had vanished like sand slipping through my fingers. *My brother, armed with deep pockets and a devious mind, leveraged his resources to manipulate the system.* ***Bribes flowed, and the authorities on duty conveniently absolved him and his accomplice, Batibat, without conducting a thorough investigation.***

Insulin murders are often described as the perfect crime—subtle, elusive, and devastatingly effective. **A single, timely C-Peptide test could have exposed the truth, but the system's inertia and corruption ensured that no such steps were taken.** I was left grappling with the bitter reality of a justice system that seemed to falter when faced with the power of money and influence.

The Fight for My Inheritance

As if the battle for my father's justice wasn't enough, I find myself entangled in yet another exhausting legal war—this time for my rightful share of my parents' properties in Mumbai and Surat. The pervasive corruption in the judicial system looms large here as well, breeding moments of despair and forcing me to question whether I will ever see the justice I seek.

Every delay, every dismissal of evidence, and every corrupt act chips away at my faith in the system. *There are days when I feel like a lone warrior in an unending war, wondering if the tide will ever turn in my favour.*

A Beacon of Hope

Yet, even in my darkest hours, when despair threatens to drown me, a gentle voice whispers to my weary soul—a voice I believe comes from the Spirit of God.

"God and His Angels are working on your behalf right now. You will see and experience advancement and growth in all areas of your life. Don't quit. Don't give up. Your breakthrough is close."

These words resonate deep within me, filling me with a renewed sense of purpose. *They remind me that, even when the road is treacherous, and the destination seems out of reach, I am not alone in this fight.*

With these words as my anchor, I rise again, determined to face whatever challenges lie ahead. My pursuit of justice is no longer just about my father or my inheritance—it has become a testament to the power of perseverance and the belief that truth, no matter how deeply buried, will ultimately come to light.

And so, I press on, fuelled by faith, hope, and an unyielding determination to see justice prevail.

Chapter 12

Embracing a New Chapter

Life, with all its twists and turns, has taught me one invaluable lesson: *my mission is not just to survive but to truly thrive.* Thriving, for me, is about embracing life with passion, extending compassion to others, laughing freely, and carrying myself with a sense of style that reflects inner confidence. The journey to this realization hasn't been straightforward, but the past few years—especially in the shadow of the COVID-19 pandemic—have been a crucible for change, pushing me to reevaluate not only my profession but also the way I interact with the world.

Transitioning to Online Practice

When the pandemic struck, like many others, I had to make difficult choices. The clinic, once a bustling hub of human connection and healing, had to close its doors temporarily. It wasn't just a safety measure; it was a necessity dictated by the times. As the months turned into years, I found myself growing increasingly comfortable with this new way of practicing medicine—virtually.

Even though the most critical phase of COVID-19 is now behind us, I've realized I have no desire to return to the clinic. My practice today is exclusively online, limited to patients I've treated for years. This isn't a matter of convenience; it's a conscious choice shaped by experience. *Modern patient behaviour, especially the habit of consulting **"Dr. Google"** before seeking professional advice, has made me question my role.* Too often, consultations feel less like collaborative problem-solving and more like a challenge to my expertise. This shift in dynamics has only deepened my resolve to focus on the patients who value and respect the doctor-patient relationship.

Protecting My Peace

At 66 years old, I have earned the right to prioritize my peace of mind. Life has gifted me with the wisdom to recognize the value of protecting my energy and avoiding unnecessary stress. As Mahatma Gandhi so eloquently put it, *"I will not allow anyone to walk through my mind with dirty feet."* These words resonate deeply with me, serving as a guiding principle in how I approach relationships and interactions.

Negativity, whether from patients, acquaintances, or even passing strangers, no longer has a place in my life. I have learned that it's not just acceptable but essential to draw boundaries. *By responding less to negativity, I am choosing to respond more to joy, gratitude, and meaningful connections.* This deliberate shift has been nothing short of transformative, making me feel lighter, freer, and more in control of my emotional landscape.

Cultivating Positivity

As I step into this new phase of life, my focus is on cultivating positivity—not just as a mind-set, but as a way of living. I firmly believe that the energy we surround ourselves with plays a crucial role in shaping our experiences. By filling my days with uplifting thoughts, meaningful conversations, and purposeful actions, I aim to manifest a life that reflects my inner aspirations.

This isn't just about me. I hope that my journey inspires others to prioritize their own well-being, to find joy in the little things, and to embrace change with courage and grace. Life is an ever-evolving story, and this chapter, for me, is about embracing the new with open arms. I choose to thrive, with compassion in my heart, laughter on my lips, and a style that is uniquely my own. *The future, with all its uncertainties, feels like a canvas waiting to be painted with vibrant colours and bold strokes. I'm ready for it.*

Chapter 13

The Journey for Redemption

A Personal Mission

My ultimate goal in life is deeply personal, yet it resonates with a Universal Truth—the Pursuit of Justice. For me, this quest is not just a fleeting desire or an ambitious dream. It is a fervent mission, one that burns in the depths of my soul and shapes every decision I make. This is about seeking justice for my father, a man who faced circumstances that demand reckoning and redress.

The path I've chosen is not an easy one. It is fraught with obstacles and dangers, but to me, it is far more meaningful than merely existing and watching life slip away under the weight of time. *I would rather dedicate my life to this noble cause, even if it costs me my own safety or comfort.* After all, our **Holy Scriptures** remind us of a vital truth: **every individual has a sacred duty to raise their voice against injustice.** And so, I march forward, driven by an unwavering resolve to fulfil this divine obligation.

The Power of Mind-set

Before anything materializes in the world around us, it begins in the silent corridors of our minds. This understanding has been one of my greatest revelations. The power of thought, belief, and perspective cannot be underestimated. It shapes reality, frames our responses, and defines our outcomes.

I have come to realize that belief in oneself is the foundation of resilience. External challenges may loom large, but they cannot shatter the spirit of someone who has cultivated an unshakeable inner confidence. Keeping the right mind-set is not just important—it is essential. *I strive to see beyond the shadows of my struggles, nurturing a vision filled with hope and clarity, knowing that better days lie ahead.*

Cultivating Inner Strength

This journey for justice has taught me the importance of developing a strong core—mentally, emotionally, and spiritually. **I've resolved to embody three guiding principles: unyielding patience, relentless positivity, and steadfast confidence in myself.** These are my shields against despair and discouragement.

Yet, I am not alone in this fight. I draw immense strength from a source far greater than myself—the Supreme Power that governs the Cosmos. This Divine Energy, this Guiding Hand, reassures me that I am not abandoned in my pursuit. With faith as my anchor, I face the uncertainties of the future with courage and determination.

The Universe's Timing

One question often echoes in my mind during quiet moments of reflection: ***Why does the Universe make me wait?*** The answer, though elusive, reveals itself in moments of clarity. The Universe operates on a timeline far grander than my limited understanding can grasp. *It sees the storms ahead, the challenges I am yet unprepared to face, and it pauses my journey to ready me for the road ahead.*

This perspective is humbling. It reminds me that waiting is not punishment but preparation. It is a gift of time—time to grow, to learn, and to strengthen myself for the battles to come.

Embracing the Wait

Learning to embrace this waiting period is no easy feat. Patience, I've come to understand, is not a passive virtue. It is an active process—a choice to trust, to hope, and to prepare while the Universe aligns the pieces of the puzzle.

This waiting, though often frustrating, is a shield that protects me from unseen perils. It is during these moments of stillness that I gather my courage, refine my skills, and deepen my understanding of the path I walk. It is a time to build resilience and fortify my spirit for the challenges that lie just beyond the horizon.

When the Universe finally deems it the right moment to act, I will be ready. Ready to seize the opportunity, to fight with all my strength, and to pursue justice with the ferocity and determination it demands.

In this journey, I remind myself daily: *waiting is not a sign of weakness. It is a testament to my commitment, my faith, and my unrelenting resolve.* **Waiting, as difficult as it may be, truly saves.**

Chapter 14

Unmasking True Colours

It is said that a person's true nature is often revealed when the pressure mounts. Over time, Dolion began to notice the relentless pursuit I had undertaken in my legal battle. The criminal case I had filed against both him and Batibat was already before the courts. Up until that point, Dolion had skilfully dodged any consequences, using his wealth and influence to bribe individuals within the Judiciary system. But despite his manipulative tactics, I was undeterred. I was committed to my mission, and I knew my unyielding resolve had been communicated to him, likely through some of our relatives—those loyal members of his network of flying monkeys.

Signs of Deception

The first crack in Dolion's carefully crafted façade appeared when he turned on one of his own—one of his flying monkeys. This particular individual, who had probably begun to see through his manipulative tactics, had reached out to me. We spoke frequently, and though we had casual conversations, I made sure to be cautious. I had educated myself extensively on narcissistic behaviour, and I knew better than to ask about Dolion or Batibat. She never volunteered any details, and I refrained from prying.

Lina, my cousin, and her husband Vinay were regular visitors at my parents' home. Even after my parents passed away, Dolion and Batibat continued to invite them over for meals, a practice that had begun years before. Vinay, a customs officer, would bring generous gifts—bottles of olive oil, whiskey, perfume, and other luxuries. These offerings ensured that Lina and Vinay were always welcomed with open arms, as they fed Dolion's need for material gain and influence.

In 2014, tragedy struck when Vinay suffered a devastating heart attack and passed away. It was during this time that Dolion's true nature began to reveal itself in full force. With no more financial benefit to gain from his relationship with Lina, he began to distance himself. Yet, he continued to try to control her. He would offer unsolicited medical advice, pushing her to take medications that were more about maintaining his power over her than about her health. Lina, a diabetic, found her blood sugar levels dangerously fluctuating after taking his recommended treatments. Despite my repeated suggestions that she consult a qualified diabetologist, Lina lacked the courage to break away. Dolion's influence extended over her entire family—her parents, her sisters, and even her children—leaving her feeling trapped.

A Fortuitous Turn

In a twist of fate, Lina contracted COVID-19 and was hospitalized. The doctor in charge reassessed her treatment and changed her medications. Finally, with proper care, Lina's blood sugar levels began to stabilize. But this was only the beginning of a much darker turn in her story, one that would shake her to her core.

Lina joined Dolion, Batibat, and her family for a trip to Ooty. It was there, in the cool hills of the Nilgiris, that everything changed. Meanwhile, I was continuing my legal efforts, sending numerous letters to Dolion concerning my rightful share of my parents' and ancestral properties. I began noticing an odd pattern of behaviour: *The Universe seemed to be sending me signs that Dolion was trying to sell off properties and escape to Australia.* As you read the chapters ahead, you'll be astounded by how these signs unfold. But what was truly shocking was that *Dolion had become convinced that it was Lina sharing information about him.*

The Ooty Incident

On the very first day of their trip to Ooty, Dolion grabbed Lina's mobile phone. As he scrolled through it, he discovered that she had made several calls to me. The realization sent him into a fit of rage. He stormed out of the room, threatening Lina with dire consequences. When Lina tried to explain that our conversations had been harmless—just discussions about recipes and places I had visited—he refused to listen. His fury only intensified, and in a moment of violent vindictiveness, **Batibat slapped Lina across the face.** Her two sisters joined in, while her mother, ever the passive bystander, said nothing. She simply watched as her eldest daughter was brutalized, too fearful or too compliant to intervene.

When Lina later recounted the incident to me, I was reminded of my own mother. Like Lina's, *my mother had never had the strength to speak up against Dolion and Batibat.* It was a heart-wrenching realization. Lina, broken and humiliated, cut her trip short and returned to Mumbai, leaving behind her mobile phone, which Dolion likely confiscated to monitor any further communications between us.

But this was not the end of Lina's torment. *Dolion unleashed his gaslighting techniques, as he had done so many times before.* He manipulated Lina's mother into disinheriting her, and he urged her younger sisters to sever all ties with her. He even poisoned Lina's sons' minds, weaving lies about their mother's "betrayals" and sowing discord within her family. He went so far as to advise the wife of Lina's younger son to avoid caring for her mother-in-law. To this day, Lina cannot comprehend what she did to deserve such cruelty. *Was it truly a crime to talk to me about innocent subjects?*

This all transpired in 2022, and I still vividly remember the devastating impact it had on Lina. Her entire family turned against her, and she spiralled into depression. I did what I could to console her, reminding her that toxic people were never worth her emotional energy. I encouraged her to see that removing these people from her life would create space for the positive forces she needed to embrace.

Moving Forward

"The people around us can be insensitive, narcissistic, toxic, and sometimes even abusive, but it is up to us to take that energy on or let it flow through us. No one is responsible for taking away our happiness, but us."

—*Aletheia Luna*

Today, despite the medical challenges she continues to face, Lina is a different person—full of life, joy, and positivity. She reflects on her past and how Dolion should have considered her circumstances. *A widowed, elderly woman, struggling with diabetes and hypertension, and reliant on a wheelchair—yet he was too self-absorbed to offer any empathy.* But narcissists, of course, are never capable of self-reflection. They always find someone else to blame for their wrongdoings.

"Narcissists are excellent actors. They know how to give a performance, mesmerizing people with their fake charm and innocence. This leaves victims feeling deflated, bewildered, and confused. It's hard to change people's perception of the narcissist because they excel at playing the victim and painting you as the abuser."

I truly believe that the Universe has a way of removing people from our lives for reasons that may not be immediately clear. Sometimes we understand those reasons years later, while other times, they remain a mystery. The important thing is to trust in the process, to trust in what the Universe has in store for us. **Trust that those who are meant to stay in our lives will remain, and those who are meant to leave will do so—regardless of the circumstances**. The Universe makes no mistakes. *Patience is key, and all we can do is trust that we are being guided toward the people and experiences that will truly serve our growth.*

Chapter 15

The Journey Begins

From the very earliest days of my life, I've carried a deep, unwavering love for travel. There's something about the idea of exploring distant, often untrodden lands, teeming with life, culture, and natural beauty, that has always fascinated me. The lure of vibrant, remote places, whether it's the rugged landscapes of the mountains or the serene solitude of untouched forests, has captivated my soul in ways that nothing else can. Nature, in its purest form, is where I find solace—far away from the chaotic hum of city life and the mass tourist crowds. While many people flock to the hustle and bustle of well-known destinations, those places have never held the same allure for me.

I have always believed that the world is like an expansive book, with each journey we take allowing us to turn a new page and experience life in all its rich diversity. It's easy to become trapped in the comfort of familiar surroundings, repeating the same routines, seeing the same faces, and reading the same pages of life. But true adventurers—those who travel—are the ones who seek to turn the page, to explore the unknown and discover what lies beyond their front doors. While many see travel as a means to escape the stresses and hardships of daily life, I have always felt differently. *We do not travel to run away from life; we travel to understand it, to peel back the layers of our identity that we may not even realize exist beneath the surface of our everyday lives.*

The Dream of Exploration

In order to fully embrace the freedom of travel, one must be fortunate enough to have both the financial resources and the time to do so. There was a time in my life when these two vital components seemed out of reach. In my previous book, I shared how, for years, my dreams of exploring the world were hampered by the lack of both time and money. But in the deepest corners of my heart, I always believed that one day—one day—I would be free. One day, I would have the opportunity to chase those dreams, to see the world that had long called to me. I would often reassure myself with the mantra, **"Someday, I will travel the world."** It was a small but powerful affirmation that helped me hold onto hope.

That *"someday"* finally arrived in 2016, when my elder son got married. This pivotal moment in my life opened up a whole new chapter. The newfound sense of freedom that came with his marriage, coupled with the resources I had gained, finally allowed me to break free from my previous limitations. It was then that I began to actively pursue the long-held dream of exploring the world.

Nathdwara: The Beginning

My very first trip was to Nathdwara, a quaint town in Rajasthan, India, famous for its ancient Shreenathji Temple, dedicated to Lord Krishna. This temple had always been close to my heart. In fact, the cover of my earlier book, **"When *He Held My Hand"***, depicts *The Blue Hand of Lord Krishna, adorned with the Sacred Om and Sudarshan Chakra.* This powerful image serves as a reminder that when a devotee sincerely prays, Divine Blessings are sent through Unseen Angels, especially in times of need. The experiences I shared in that book were born from these deeply personal beliefs, offering readers a glimpse into the spiritual truths I hold dear.

The journey to Nathdwara, however, didn't unfold quite as I had imagined. During my son's wedding, my aunt from Bharuch (a city in Gujarat) had promised to accompany me on this trip, a gesture that filled me with great excitement. After all, it had been over 15 years since I had ventured beyond Mumbai, aside from a few brief trips to Pune for school. Nathdwara, with its deep spiritual significance, seemed like the perfect destination to begin my travels. But when the time came, my aunt backed out. She cited her daughter's concerns about her back problems as the reason, though curiously, she later made several trips to Nathdwara on her own. I was disappointed, to say the least, but my desire to receive Lord Krishna's blessings never waned.

A Friend's Support

Just when I thought my journey would be delayed indefinitely, a dear friend of mine, Vanya, came to my rescue. Upon hearing my story, Vanya, without a second thought, promised to accompany me on this long-awaited pilgrimage. Within just two days, we found ourselves on the road to Nathdwara, our hearts filled with anticipation. The blessings we received from Lord Krishna during that visit became the foundation of a travel adventure that would last for years to come. *This journey marked the beginning of a new chapter in my life—one of exploration, growth, and spiritual awakening.*

Though my travels were momentarily halted by the global pandemic in 2020, I didn't let that stop me. I patiently waited for the world to heal, knowing that when the time was right, I would continue my adventures. In 2021, I returned to my travels with renewed enthusiasm and a deep sense of gratitude. Each new place I visited, each new experience I encountered, brought me closer to understanding both the world and my place within it. *The journey, I realized, wasn't just about the destinations—it was about the lessons learned, the connections made, and the moments of reflection along the way.*

Chapter 16

The Travel Bug

Once the travel bug bites, there is no known antidote, and for me, it became a delightful affliction that I have embraced with open arms. From 2016 onwards, a deep wanderlust took hold of my life, driving me to embark on countless journeys. These adventures took me not only across the diverse and mesmerizing landscapes of India but also to distant corners of the world. *Every trip has been a blessing, a treasure trove of memories that I will carry with me forever.*

One of the most incredible opportunities during this period came courtesy of my elder son, who worked for an airline affiliated with Air India. Thanks to this, I had the privilege of flying in luxurious Business Class, an experience I would never have dreamed of otherwise. Imagine this: reclining comfortably at 35,000 feet, savouring gourmet meals, and being treated like royalty. The only cost was the minimal airport taxes my son had to pay. It was as if the universe had conspired to make my dreams of exploring the world come true. Truly, **A Divine Blessing!**

Solo Adventures: Freedom and Self-Discovery

While some might shy away from traveling alone, I found it exhilarating and empowering. Solo travel gave me the unparalleled freedom to chart my own course. I could choose where to go, how long to stay, what to eat, and what experiences to indulge in, without the need to consider anyone else's preferences.

Each journey became an intimate dialogue between me and the world. I wandered through ancient ruins, strolled along serene beaches, and tasted exotic cuisines that tantalized my taste buds. Whether it was sitting quietly in a quaint café in Amalfi Coast in Italy or watching the sun dip below the horizon in Kerala, these moments were mine alone. They were precious, liberating, and deeply fulfilling.

The Dynamics of Group Travel

While I relished traveling solo, I also had the opportunity to explore the dynamics of group travel. One of the most memorable experiences was when I led a group of 30 people to the iconic Statue of Unity in Kevadia, Gujarat. As a manager and guide for this trip, I gained a unique perspective on the challenges faced by senior citizens.

Many in the group were reliant on their children and seemed hesitant about venturing beyond their comfort zones. Their stories revealed lives shaped by dependence, caution, and the kind of wisdom that only comes with age. It was a humbling experience to see how differently people approach travel based on their circumstances. For some, this trip was a rare adventure, while for others, it was a way to reconnect with the world.

Lessons from the Road

Travel has a way of teaching lessons that no classroom ever could. It opens your eyes to the beauty of diversity, the resilience of the human spirit, and the universality of emotions. Each journey introduced me to new faces and fascinating stories, whether it was a local artisan in Chandigarh or a fellow traveller in Langkawi. These encounters enriched my understanding of life and broadened my perspective.

Travel is often said to be the only thing you buy that makes you richer, and I couldn't agree more. It has been my greatest teacher, offering not just joy and adventure, but also a profound connection to the world around me. Whether wandering alone or exploring with others, every trip has been a step closer to understanding myself and the beautiful, complex tapestry of humanity.

And so, with the travel bug firmly in my soul, I continue to embrace the world, one journey at a time.

Chapter 17

The Allure Of Lahaul and Spiti Valley

"I would rather own a little and see the world than own the world and see a little bit."
— Alexandra Sattler

My Journey to Spiti: A Daring Adventure

Among all the enchanting destinations I have explored in India, Lahaul and Spiti Valley hold a special place in my heart. These valleys are not merely scenic wonders; they are daring, uncharted realms that challenge both the body and the soul. Back in 2017, Spiti was far from being a mainstream destination. Its roads were rugged and treacherous, and its name often elicited blank stares from those unfamiliar with this hidden paradise. Whenever my friends or colleagues inquired about it, I would patiently explain, *"It's near Leh and Ladakh."* But unlike the bustling tourist hubs of Leh and Ladakh, Lahaul and Spiti remained pristine, untouched by commercial tourism, their allure almost secretive.

Even before setting foot in Spiti, I had seen videos of its infamous roads. Narrow, twisting, and bordered by sheer cliffs, they seemed more like a daredevil's challenge than a travel route. I vividly recall the mix of excitement and dread I felt as I prepared for my journey. There were moments when I genuinely questioned my decision—especially after convincing myself I might not return to Mumbai alive! To mitigate my anxiety (and my family's concerns), I took out a hefty premium life insurance policy. Ironically, I ended up cancelling it soon after returning, realizing I couldn't sustain the financial burden of the quarterly premium. That adventure, however, left me with an unshakable belief: **life is a daring adventure, or it is nothing at all.**

Spiti Valley: Then and Now

Fast forward to today, and Spiti Valley has undergone a transformation. The roads are far better, no longer life-threatening, and accessible to a broader audience. Tour operators now prominently feature Spiti in their itineraries, showcasing its raw beauty to an ever-growing number of travellers. Yet, even amidst its newfound popularity, Spiti retains its essence—a jewel of India, waiting to be discovered by those who crave the extraordinary.

The Mummy Of Gue: A Fascinating Discovery

One of the most fascinating treasures of Spiti Valley lies in the remote village of Gue: *the 593-year-old mummy of Sangha Tenzing.* This Buddhist monk from Tibet remains preserved in a meditative posture, his skin, hair, and nails still intact. **He is the only known monk in India to have achieved self-mummification**—a practice as mysterious as it is inspiring. Sangha Tenzing willingly underwent this ritual at the age of 36, a story that captured my imagination and pushed me to think deeper about life, purpose, and legacy.

Birth Of My YouTube Channel

This extraordinary tale of the monk became the inspiration for my YouTube channel, which I affectionately named **"Travel and Motivational Channel."** Through this platform, I sought to share the wonders of the world with others, especially those who, for various reasons, could not travel themselves. Every destination has a story, and I wanted to narrate these tales—not just as a travelogue, but as a source of inspiration.

The Mission Behind My Channel

The channel became a space where I could blend my two passions: exploring uncharted territories and uplifting people with meaningful stories. For me, travel isn't just about ticking destinations off a list; it's about uncovering hidden lessons, connecting with new cultures, and growing as a person. My videos aim to transport viewers to these magical places, offering them not just visuals but also narratives enriched with history, culture, and morality.

The ultimate goal of my channel isn't fame or followers—it's impact. If even one story or one video motivates someone to become a better version of themselves, I will consider my efforts worthwhile. After all, knowledge and experiences are not meant to be hoarded. As the saying goes, *"No matter how much knowledge you gain, it is useless unless you share it and let it spread like light."*

Lessons from Spiti Valley

Spiti Valley taught me many things, but most of all, it reminded me that *the world is full of wonders, waiting to be discovered by those brave enough to venture beyond their comfort zones.* And in **sharing those discoveries, we become part of a chain of inspiration that connects us all.**

Chapter 18

A Journey of Miracles

"Believe in miracles. I have seen so many of them come when every other indication would say that hope was lost. Hope is never lost."
— *Jeffrey R. Holland*

Life has a way of surprising us, often when we least expect it. Sometimes, these surprises are so profound, so otherworldly, that they leave an indelible mark on our hearts and minds. This is the story of one such moment—*a miracle that unfolded during a spiritual pilgrimage in May 2022, reshaping my understanding of life, faith, and the Extraordinary Power of the Divine.*

The Pilgrimage Begins

In the summer of 2022, I set out on the Char Dham Yatra, a Mini Char Dham, to be precise, a revered Hindu pilgrimage that had long been on my bucket list. This sacred journey takes devotees to four holy shrines nestled in the Indian Himalayas—Yamunotri, Gangotri, Kedarnath, and Badrinath. Each destination holds its own spiritual significance, collectively symbolizing a path toward self-discovery and divine connection.

I wasn't alone on this quest. Accompanying me was my childhood friend Daksha, a steadfast partner in many adventures, and a trusted tour operator, Apna Bharat Pravas, who managed the logistics of our trip. The journey began smoothly, with our visits to Yamunotri and Gangotri filled with moments of awe and quiet reflection. But little did I know, **Kedarnath—the third destination—would be the site of an encounter that would alter the very fabric of my soul.**

Kedarnath: The Sacred Abode

Kedarnath Temple, an ancient shrine dedicated to Lord Shiva, is a place steeped in spirituality and legend. Located at an altitude of 11,755 feet, it is cradled by snow-capped peaks in the Garhwal Himalayan Range. The temple's history spans over 1,200 years, making it one of the most revered sites in Hinduism. Accessible only between April and November, Kedarnath draws countless pilgrims each year, their faith unwavering despite the arduous journey. Due to the harsh winters, the temple is closed during the remaining six months. The deity of the temple is carried down to Ukhimath, to be worshipped during those severe cold six months.

Post Covid, after a span of 2 years, all temples were opened for darshan to the public. Hence in May 2022, the number of tourists at every destination especially the religious places had increased by many folds. Kedarnath was no different. The throngs of devotees were overwhelming, and resources like dolis (palanquins) and ponies were scarce. Left with no choice, I opted for a kandi—a sling-like carrier borne on the shoulders of a porter. The seven-hour ascent was gruelling yet uneventful, leaving me unprepared for what awaited at the summit.

A Miraculous Encounter

Upon arriving in Kedarnath, I reached out to Yogeshji, a temple Pujari (priest) with connections to my family. My maternal uncle always helped him during difficult times, and Yogesh's gratitude was evident in his warm hospitality. He greeted me like his niece, guiding me to the modest hotel where I was scheduled to stay with Daksha and a couple from Hyderabad, Tilak and Aparna.

Something peculiar happened that evening. Despite the reported crowds, the streets appeared eerily empty as I walked to the hotel. *Though my eyes were open, I could not see a single human being. It felt as though the Universe had carved a path just for me, wrapping the town in a blanket of serenity.*

Kedarnath temple is open to the public for the entire 24 hours. Pooja can be done inside the temple, by the pujari, for the devotees, only at 2.30 am. Hence, at 2:30 a.m., Yogesh Maharaj arrived at my room. He applied some oil on my forehead, and removed my shoes, socks, gloves and monkey cap. He guided me towards the temple for the special pooja (ritual). Strangely, I was convinced it was 6:00

a.m., a disorienting discrepancy that seemed trivial at that time. As we approached the temple, the silence of the night was almost deafening. *Where were the thousands of devotees I'd heard about?* Only scene my eyes could see was the temple covered in snow. In reality, the Kedarnath temple never gets covered in snow even in the harshest of winters!

Daksha told me later, that in the biting cold she was shocked to see me walking towards the temple barefoot, and minus my gloves and monkey cap.

I distinctly remember entering the temple from the side entrance. Inside the temple, my breath caught. Before me stood the triangular Jyotirlinga, bathed in a soft, otherworldly light. As instructed by Yogeshji, I knelt and embraced the Shivling. At that moment, an overwhelming presence enveloped me. **I looked up, and there He was— Lord Shiva Himself, His gaze piercing yet comforting.** Time stood still as I felt an indescribable connection, a profound assurance that I was not alone.

The Aftermath

When I finally rose, Yogeshji led me to the temple's verandah, where I sat in a trance-like state for what felt like an eternity. Daksha and Tilak, worried by my unresponsiveness, called out to me repeatedly. Their voices barely registered, as if muffled by an invisible barrier. *They thought that they had lost me.* Finally, in a desperate bid to bring me back, *Tilak placed his hand on my head and*

began chanting "Har Har Mahadev" 108 times, with unwavering devotion. I have no memory of this either.

I was told later that I sat in the verandah for almost an hour with my eyes open, but I was not responding to any of words uttered by those around. I remember being taken to my room thereafter. The same scene... I could not see a single human being. Yogeshji, sensing my fragile condition, swiftly arranged for a helicopter to take me downhill. *This was nothing short of miraculous; securing a helicopter seat during peak season, especially post-COVID, was nearly impossible.* Yet, somehow, it happened.

As I was escorted to the helipad, the crowds returned, bustling and chaotic as if the spell of solitude had lifted. I was flown to the base, then transported to a nearby hotel, where I collapsed into a deep, unbroken sleep for over 24 hours.

When I finally awoke, I felt... different. Lighter, freer, and profoundly grateful. *The experience had stripped away my doubts, leaving behind a clarity that was both humbling and empowering.*

A New Beginning

This journey to Kedarnath was more than a pilgrimage; it was a revelation. The miraculous events I witnessed reaffirmed my faith in the unseen forces that govern our lives. *They reminded me of the vastness of the universe and our small, yet significant, place within it.*

I carry this story with me not as proof of the divine, but as a testament to the mysteries that surround us. In a world often dominated by logic and reason, moments like these invite us to believe in something greater—a force that binds us all in ways we may never fully comprehend.

"Maybe miracles are given not to prove anything but simply to remind us that the physical world is not as solid and real and dependable as we think."
— Dwight Longenecker

Chapter 19

Signs from the Universe

"The Universe is always speaking to us, sending us little messages, causing coincidences and serendipities, reminding us to stop, to look around, to believe in something else, something more."
— Nancy Thayer

The Universe's Subtle Signs

Life is an intricate dance of energy, often leading us to unexpected places. The world around us is not as random as it may seem; it's a symphony of connections, weaving together people, events, and moments that align with the energy we project. The Universe whispers to us in ways both subtle and profound—through coincidences that make us pause, through synchronicities that nudge us forward, and through serendipities that remind us of life's wonder. *These signs aren't just chance occurrences; they are messages, invitations to trust in something bigger, to believe in a grander design.*

As I transitioned from my offline medical practice to an uncertain future, I found myself caught in the liminal space between the past and possibility. The question of what to do with my clinic loomed large: Should I sell it or lease it out? I uploaded its details to a property app, expressing my desire for any of the options. Depending on the offer, I would decide to sell or rent my clinic. I was sure that this digital sphere might offer a solution.

A Cosmic Nudge

And then, out of the blue, a notification flashed across my screen: **"4BHK Apartment for Sale in Swaraj Housing Society, Vile Parle."**

The 4BHK was for sale for a whopping 20 crores INR. There was a video showing the 2 flats fully furnished. *The advertisement read that the 4BHK was for sale as it is.* It meant that it included furniture and electronic items also. It struck me that **only if someone is migrating, he sells outright everything in his apartment.** I said to myself, *"I must put an obstacle in this sale"*.

It wasn't just an advertisement—it felt like a cosmic nudge, as though the Universe was drawing my attention to something important.

Navigating Uncertainty

Yet, even as the signs pointed me in intriguing directions, I couldn't shake the cloud of apprehension hovering over me. What if Dolion and Batibat managed to flee to Australia before the court hearings? How would justice find its way to them if they were no longer here? My uneasy feeling deepened since I was aware that the new Secretary and Chairman of Swaraj Housing Cooperative Society had been ensnared in Dolion's web of lies and deceit. *They had joined Dolion's clan of flying monkeys.* His charisma, coupled with extravagant gifts, had won them over, ensuring their cooperation. With allies like them, obtaining a no objection certificate (NOC) to sell the flats would be effortless for Dolion.

It felt like a cruel twist of fate. How could the same Universe that whispered signs of alignment also allow such blatant deceit? Yet, I reminded myself: that the Universe rarely provides straightforward answers. It sends us challenges to grow our strength and signs to guide our steps.

Taking Action

The urgency of the situation spurred me into action. I couldn't sit idly by while Dolion schemed to dispose of properties that held such deep significance for my family. I immediately contacted my lawyer, Sunil, who prepared and issued a legal notice to the society. The notice explicitly stated that **I, as my parents' daughter, held a rightful claim to the two flats.** *It also warned that any issuance of an NOC without my written consent would result in criminal charges against the society's Secretary and Chairman.*

The flats were more than bricks and mortar to me—they were symbols of my family's history and struggles. One of them had belonged to my mother, who had been manipulated into handing it over to Batibat. I had chronicled that painful chapter in my first book, **"When He Held My**

Hand," detailing the emotional and psychological abuse Dolion inflicted on her. The second flat had been purchased by my father but was registered in my uncle's name. My father had earlier purchased a flat in his own name in Bhayandar (a suburb of Mumbai). He had given it to his brother to stay with his family. My paternal uncle was not doing well financially. He did not even have a decent job either to purchase a flat for his family or to feed them two decent meals a day. My father had stepped in during his brother's lean phase. Not only did he give him a place to stay with his family, but he also gave him money and adequate groceries every month to feed his entire family. In the latter chapters, *I have disclosed the cunning and manipulative role played by this same paternal uncle. It is shocking how greed still continues to consume him at the age of 90 years!* My father had often spoken to me about these two flats, assuring me that it would one day rightfully be mine.

Unveiling the Deception

What came next felt like a gut punch. Dolion had audaciously forged signatures—including those of the society's Chairman and Secretary—to place his name on the share certificate of the flat standing in my uncle's name, which actually was purchased by my father's money. Holding the Xerox copy of the document in my hands, I was appalled by the sheer audacity of his deceit. It wasn't just a legal battle I was stepping into; it was a battle for truth, justice, and my family's legacy.

As daunting as it all felt, I reminded myself of the signs. The Universe had brought me to this moment, not to overwhelm me, but to prepare me. With my father's whispered blessings in my heart and the quiet assurance of the Universe's guidance, I knew I was ready. The road ahead would be fraught with challenges, but I was determined to stand my ground and fight for what was rightfully mine.

Every step forward felt like an affirmation of trust—in myself, in the justice system, and in the subtle, persistent whispers of the Universe.

Chapter 20

The Power of Intuition

The Whisper of Truth

Intuition is often regarded as a mysterious, almost magical force—a Superpower of sorts. For those who tune into it, intuition feels like an innate compass, guiding us through the fog of uncertainty. Often described as gut feelings, it's a voice beyond logic—a whisper from the depths of our soul. This voice, free from the constraints of fear and doubt, seeks to steer us toward paths we might not dare tread otherwise. *It is our soul's earnest attempt to nudge us closer to truth, purpose, and clarity.*

One chilly November morning, as I sipped my tea, a thought cut through the hum of everyday distractions. It was sharp and unsettling, like an arrow to the mind: *If Dolion and Batibat, my brother and sister-in-law, were planning to migrate, Dolion might try to sell my grandfather's bungalow in Surat.* My heart tightened at the possibility. My father, who had inherited the bungalow, had once let slip that he hadn't made a will. This meant that *I, as his daughter, had a rightful claim to a share of this ancestral property.*

As the thought took root, it became impossible to ignore the undeniable: Dolion's obsession with property and money was consuming him. He had a history of prioritizing financial gain over family ties, but this—this felt like a new low.

The idea of traveling to Surat after nearly 30 years filled me with apprehension. Memories of the city were distant and faint, like pages from an old diary. Questions swirled in my mind: *Where would I stay? Who could I turn to for help? What if this journey unearthed truths I wasn't ready to face?* Yet, amidst the uncertainty, there was a quiet voice within me insisting I go.

A Leap of Faith

As doubt threatened to overtake me, I remembered a line I'd read years ago: *"If you are willing to do the work with God, He will bless your life in ways you have never dreamed."* It resonated deeply. While we cannot rewrite the past, faith gives us the courage to shape our future.

Guided by this belief, I made the decision. I booked a train ticket to Surat, reserved a modest hotel room, and packed a small bag. I didn't know how long I would stay or what I would encounter, but one thing was clear: I had to go.

Two days later, I arrived in Surat. The city had grown and changed, yet there was an air of familiarity in its bustling streets. After settling into the hotel, I hailed an auto-rickshaw and made my way to my grandfather's bungalow.

Unveiling Deceit

The Silent House and the Old Man

The sight that greeted me was disheartening. The once-vibrant house now stood silent, its doors ajar, as if mourning its past. Inside, an old man sat on the floor of an empty room. His presence felt strangely symbolic, as though he had been placed there by fate to unveil the truth I sought.

The Shocking Sale and The Betrayal

The man welcomed me graciously and confirmed my fears: **his nephew had purchased the bungalow for a staggering one crore rupees**. The transaction was complete. My heart sank as I revealed my identity and my rightful claim. He was stunned. **Dolion, he explained, had portrayed himself as the sole heir, concealing my existence entirely.**

As we spoke, he shared another shocking revelation. *Dolion had promised to leave the furniture intact as part of the sale agreement. Yet, when the new owners moved in, they found the bungalow stripped bare—right down to the tube lights, fans, and water pump.* ***Even in betrayal, my brother had spared no opportunity for gain.***

The Role of my Cousin

The depth of deception didn't end there. My cousin, who lived next door, had played a role in this betrayal. *For a mere two lakh rupees as commission, he had witnessed the sale deed and signed an affidavit where Dolion falsely declared himself as my parents' only child.* My cousin's ID and signature on the sale deed would later confirm his complicity.

The Bitter Taste of Betrayal

Before leaving, I encountered my cousin and his wife outside their home. They invited me in for tea, their hospitality laced with a veneer of innocence. When I questioned them about the sale deed, they dodged my inquiries with rehearsed ignorance. Yet, the truth was undeniable; the evidence was in the documents I would soon obtain.

As I walked away, anger and sadness mingled in my chest. I couldn't help but recall the words of a wise man: *"Money is the worst discovery of human life, but it is the most trusted material to test human nature."* In those moments, I saw the truth of it reflected in my own family.

Money—a simple creation of humankind—wields immense power. It can corrupt even the most sacred bonds, erode trust, and turn kin into strangers. How had it come to hold such sway over our lives? I pondered this as I stood outside the bungalow, the weight of the truth settling over me.

The journey was far from over. As I write this, I know there is much more to uncover and battles yet to be fought. **But one thing is certain: this chapter of betrayal will shape the chapters to come.**

Chapter 21

Vacation Tales and Acts of Kindness

In the vibrant city of Surat, nestled beside my grandfather's charming bungalow, stood a beautiful home owned by a Parsi family. This house wasn't just another neighbourly residence; it held a personal connection that made it even more special. The owners were the sisters and mother of my school friend Urvi's mother. This serendipitous link added a layer of warmth to our already treasured family vacations.

My school breaks—be it Diwali, Christmas, or the long, balmy summer days—were almost always spent at my grandfather's bungalow. It was a time of pure joy, free from the weight of schoolwork and responsibilities. As fate would have it, Urvi also spent her vacations at her grandmother's place next door. What began as a happy coincidence soon became a tradition, forging a bond between us that transformed us from mere acquaintances into inseparable vacation friends.

Minal: A Pillar of the Neighbourhood

Urvi's family was cared for by a kind-hearted woman named Minal. But Minal was far more than just a caregiver—she was the heartbeat of our little community. Her dedication went beyond her household duties, as she also served as the neighbourhood's beloved milk supplier.

In those simpler times, milk was delivered in glass bottles, each sealed with an aluminium cap. The bottles themselves were a reflection of an era where life seemed less rushed and more thoughtful. Every evening, families would leave their empty bottles in cloth bags outside their doors, a quiet ritual signalling trust and routine. By morning, Minal would have replaced them with fresh, bottles of milk. Whether it was whole milk or toned, the system worked seamlessly, almost like magic to my young eyes.

The memory of Minal's quiet efficiency and her warm presence remains a cherished piece of my childhood. She embodied the essence of community—reliable, nurturing, and deeply connected to everyone around her.

A Tapestry of Memories

The memories of my vacations in Surat are like an intricate tapestry woven with laughter, warmth, and adventure. Urvi and I spent our days exploring the lush gardens that framed our homes. We played hide-and-seek among the trees, picked guavas fresh from the branches, and spent countless afternoons sipping on the sweet, cooling chaas that Minal would lovingly prepare for us.

Evenings were magical in their simplicity. As the sun dipped below the horizon, casting a golden glow across the bungalows, we would sit on the porch and share our dreams, fears, and secrets. The festivals were the highlight of our time together—each celebration an explosion of colour, music, and joy that brought us closer not just as friends but as extensions of each other's families.

Looking back, those moments weren't just vacations; they were life lessons wrapped in joy. They taught me about the richness of friendship, the beauty of traditions, and the profound impact of shared experiences. Each memory is a thread in the fabric of my childhood, bright and unbreakable.

A Generous Legacy

Life took its course, and after the passing of Urvi's grandmother and her two aunts, a remarkable gesture followed. ***Urvi's mother made the decision to gift their bungalow to Minal, recognizing the selfless care and unwavering dedication she had shown to the family over the years.***

This act of kindness was more than just a transfer of property; it was a testament to gratitude, trust, and the enduring bonds that go beyond blood relations. **In a world often consumed by material pursuits, this gesture stood out as a shining example of humanity at its finest.** It reminded us all of the profound truth that real wealth lies in the relationships we nurture and the love we give.

Minal, who had given so much of herself to the family, was now being given something that truly belonged to her—a home she had helped sustain with her care and devotion. *This act wasn't just about fairness; it was about recognizing the human connection that turns strangers into family.*

Reflections and Comparisons

Reflecting on this generosity, I couldn't help but draw a comparison to my own family. My brother Dolion often comes to mind during these moments of introspection. His actions—or sometimes the lack thereof—highlight the stark contrast between individuals driven by rules and those guided by a moral compass.

Urvi's mother didn't act out of obligation; she acted out of an intrinsic understanding of what was right. Her decision echoed the wisdom that good people don't need laws to dictate their behaviour—they simply follow their hearts and values. *On the other hand, the harsh reality remains that those (like Dolion) who lack such a compass often find ways to circumvent rules, a reminder of the complexities of human nature.*

Lessons in a Time of Chaos

In a world that often feels dominated by self-interest and negativity, stories like these shine as beacons of hope. They remind us that goodness is not extinct; it just requires quiet strength and unwavering integrity. Urvi's mother's decision wasn't grandiose or showy, but its impact was profound.

Her actions encourage us to think deeply about our own choices and the legacy we wish to leave behind. ***In the midst of Kalyug—a time marked by chaos and strife—such acts of kindness are a reminder that the power to bring light into the world lies within each of us.***

Every small act of generosity, every moment of empathy, and every decision made with love creates ripples that extend far beyond our immediate circles. These are the values I hope to carry forward, inspired by the simple yet profound gestures of those around me. *They remind us that even in the most challenging times, we can choose to be kind, to act with integrity, and to leave the world a little better than we found it.*

Chapter 22

A Fortuitous Encounter

November 2023 found me wandering through the familiar streets of my childhood, lost in thought. The air carried the faint aroma of nostalgia, a blend of past memories and present realities. Each step felt heavy, weighted by the bittersweet news that had occupied my mind—the sale of my grandfather's beloved bungalow, a cherished symbol of our family's legacy. It was this poignant mix of emotions that prompted me to make a courtesy call to Minal, an old acquaintance who lived nearby.

The decision was impulsive, but as soon as I stepped into her home, I was met with warmth and familiarity. Minal greeted me with open arms, her effusive energy dispelling the years that had passed since our last meeting. I was meeting her after approximately 30 years, but still she recognized me. Her kindness was matched only by her perceptiveness; she was already aware of my grandfather's bungalow sale. She quickly turned the conversation toward the subject which was weighing heavily in my mind after hearing about the sale, of my ancestral bungalow, by

Dolion. She urged me, with heartfelt conviction, to assert my rights over the ancestral property.

Unexpected Guidance

As we sat deep in discussion, a second Minal—coincidentally sharing the same name—entered the house. She had come to assist with household chores, but her arrival felt far from ordinary. Her timing was impeccable, as if choreographed by the universe. Just as I confided in Minal 1 about my struggles, lamenting the lack of trustworthy legal counsel in Surat, Minal 2 listened intently, her demeanour shifting with purpose.

Then, with quiet certainty, she spoke, claiming to be guided by a voice from a Supreme Power. Her message was direct: *I needed to meet a lawyer named Advocate Jitesh.* Scepticism crept into my voice as I expressed my concerns. How could I, with limited resources, possibly find a lawyer who would not be swayed by the immense wealth and influence of Dolion? But Minal 2 was resolute, her confidence unshaken. She assured me that *Advocate Jitesh was a man of integrity, someone incorruptible and driven by principles. There wasn't even an iota of chance that Dolion would be able to bribe him.*

Divine Intervention

The encounter left me both bewildered and hopeful, as though I had stumbled into the realm of Divine Intervention. Life has a way of presenting us with choices and signs, often when we least expect them. At that moment, it felt as though unseen forces were at play, orchestrating events to guide me through a challenge I thought insurmountable.

Looking back, the sequence of events that day carried an undeniable air of serendipity:

1) **The spontaneous visit**:

A simple decision to stop by Minal 1's house turned into a life-altering moment.

2) **The perfectly timed arrival**:

Minal 2 entered just when our conversation had reached a critical juncture.

3) **A pivotal introduction**:

Her certainty about Advocate Jitesh transformed my hopelessness into a cautious optimism.

Each detail felt too precise to be mere coincidence. It was as though the universe was reminding me that even in our darkest hours, there are forces at work, weaving threads of hope and guidance into the fabric of our lives.

A Quiet Reminder

This moment added another chapter to my belief in the mysterious ways life unfolds. Time and again, I have found myself at crossroads, unsure of the way forward, only to be nudged gently in the right direction by unseen hands. These encounters, though fleeting, reaffirm my faith in the Power of the Universe to provide what we need, just when we need it most.

As I prepared to meet Advocate Jitesh, I couldn't help but feel a quiet sense of reassurance. *Perhaps, just perhaps, this was the beginning of justice unfolding, not by sheer effort but by a fortuitous alignment of circumstances.*

Chapter 23

A Message to My Dad

"Dad, I know you are in Heaven, always watching over me, and that your guiding hand will be forever on my shoulder."

These words are not just a fleeting sentiment but my constant source of comfort, my bridge to you across the vast expanse of existence. They remind me that love transcends the physical and that your presence remains, even if unseen.

I often find myself speaking to you in quiet moments, seeking your wisdom in times of doubt. Your voice, though now a memory, has never truly faded. It echoes in my heart, offering strength when I falter.

A Surprising Encounter

On the insistence of Minal 2, I scheduled an appointment with Advocate Jitesh. At first, it felt like just another errand in my seemingly endless quest for justice. But when I walked into his office, the strangest thing happened—his voice stopped me in my tracks. It was startlingly similar to my father's, as though the Universe had orchestrated this encounter to remind me that I was not alone in this battle.

It felt like hearing an old, cherished voice, one that carried both comfort and sorrow. It was uncanny and a little unsettling, yet it also filled me with a sense of hope. The thought crossed my mind: ***"Sometimes, the dead speak louder than the living."*** It was as if my father had found a way to guide me, even through a stranger.

Seeking Clarity

When I arrived at Advocate Jitesh's office, I was completely unprepared. I had no documents, no clear plan, and no idea how to proceed. My mind was a whirlwind of doubts and fears. But then I remembered Ash Alves' wise words:

"You are not always going to have the answer to your problems. It may take time for you to gain clarity over the situation. Instead of endless worrying, allow Divine Intervention to ease the anxieties. Have faith that clarity will be found over time."

These words were my anchor. I took a deep breath and allowed myself to trust the process, to believe that answers would come when they were meant to.

Sharing My Story

As I sat across from Advocate Jitesh, I poured out my story, every detail, every injustice. He listened intently, his expression a mix of empathy and quiet determination. It was clear that he was not just a man of the law but a man of principles, someone who genuinely cared about justice.

It didn't take him long to understand the situation. *"Dolion,"* he said, *"is cunning and self-serving. People like him exploit loopholes and take advantage of others. But don't worry. We'll fight this together."* His words felt like a promise, one that brought a sense of relief I hadn't felt in a long time.

To my surprise, he offered to take on my case for a minimal fee. His junior, Advocate Kanha, also pledged to work tirelessly to secure justice for me. It was a moment of gratitude so profound that I silently thanked both Minals for leading me to this extraordinary lawyer.

The Civil Suit

True to his word, within days, Advocate Jitesh filed a civil suit against both Dolion and the new owner, Mr. Pratap. When I questioned why Mr. Pratap was included, his explanation was meticulous and clear:

"As per the law, the new owner is responsible for obtaining proper title clearance. If that had been done correctly, you would not have been deprived of your rightful share. Your grandfather's bungalow was willed to your father, and by extension, to both of you as his children. It's not legally possible for the entire payment to have been made to your brother without your knowledge or consent."

His words were a revelation, shedding light on the layers of deceit that had been woven around me.

The Power of Intuition

Reflecting on the events that led me to this point, I couldn't help but marvel at the Power of Intuition. It was almost as if the Universe had whispered in my ear, urging me to pay attention, to dig deeper, to act. That fleeting sense of unease, that inexplicable feeling that something was wrong—it turned out to be my greatest ally.

It's true what they say:

"Trust your Intuition. It never lies. Intuition is your soul whispering the truth to your heart and hoping that you hear."

Perhaps it was Divine Intervention or the silent guidance of my father, but one thing was clear—I was no longer alone in this fight. *Justice was no longer a distant dream but a tangible goal, and for the first time in years, I felt the stirrings of hope.*

Chapter 24

The Right to Information

The ***Right to Information*** (RTI) is not just a law; it's a tool of empowerment for every Indian citizen. It grants people the right to access information from government offices, departments, ministries, and even organizations substantially funded by the government. *The essence of RTI lies in its ability to bring transparency, foster accountability, and curb corruption, enabling citizens to actively participate in the democratic process. It is a bridge that connects ordinary individuals to the functioning of government machinery, ensuring that no injustice goes unnoticed.*

Before I met Advocate Jitesh, I had already taken my first step in utilizing this powerful instrument. I filed an RTI application to uncover a crucial piece of my family's story: the sale deed of my grandfather's bungalow. The property card, obtained through this application, unveiled a vital detail — ***my grandfather's will from 1986 had clearly bequeathed the bungalow to my father. There was no subsequent will to alter this arrangement, which meant that legally, the property was rightfully owned by my brother and me.***

Yet, in 2022, Dolion sold the bungalow, claiming sole ownership based on documents he had submitted to the city survey office in 2021. This betrayal cut deep, not just because of the property but because of the deceit it represented.

A Spark of Determination

The words of John Lewis echoed in my mind:

"When you see something that is not right, not fair, not just, you have to speak up, you have to say something, you have to do something."

Motivated by this wisdom, I resolved to uncover the truth. My next RTI application was directed at the city survey office in Surat, where I sought the documents Dolion had submitted to claim the bungalow.

Uncovering the Deception

What I discovered left me breathless. Dolion had filed a **sworn affidavit** falsely declaring himself as the sole child of my parents. This was no mere oversight; it was a calculated act of fraud. **To cover his tracks, Dolion bribed a city survey officer, to the tune of Rs. 2 lakhs, to hide the affidavit within the files from 2002, making it appear unrelated to the 2021 sale.** His plan was clear: if I ever came searching, the officer could claim the papers were missing, closing the case.

But **Fate**—or perhaps the **"Hand of God"**—intervened. A diligent and honest clerk at the survey office unearthed the hidden file. This document exposed Dolion's treachery and revealed the staggering betrayal: he had sold the bungalow for ₹**1 crore**, stripping me of my rightful inheritance.

The Fight for Justice

As I held the documents in my trembling hands, a storm of emotions raged within me—anger, grief, and a fiery determination. *How could such blatant injustice go unanswered? Why should I and my children be deprived of our rightful share?*

*Dolion's children stood to inherit everything, while mine were being left with nothing. Was this fair? Was this just? The answer was clear—**it was not.***

This was no longer just a legal battle; it was a fight for justice, for my rights, and for the legacy of my family. Armed with the power of RTI, the truth, and an unshakable resolve, I vowed to see this through.

Justice may be delayed, but it cannot be denied. This was my fight—not just for a bungalow but for the values my family had stood for: honesty, fairness, and the courage to confront wrongdoing. **The battle was on.**

Chapter 25

The Strength of Resolve

A Call for Integrity and Justice

"Continue to speak out against all forms of injustice to yourself and others, and you will set a mighty example for your children and for future generations."
— *Bernice King*

With The Document clenched in my hands like a shield, I approached the authorities, my heart resolute. My application was meticulous, a testimony of my unwavering determination to seek justice. *Dolion's false affidavit, filed with malicious intent, was not just a lie—it was a criminal act. I vowed to see him face the consequences.*

The law in India is explicit: **when a civil case involves a criminal offense, the police must register a First Information Report (FIR).** My spirits soared as the authorities appeared supportive, reassuring me that once the local police completed their investigation, charges would be brought against Dolion. I whispered a prayer of gratitude, feeling a rare glimmer of hope.

The Frustrating Wait

But justice, it seemed, moved at a glacial pace. Days turned into weeks, and weeks into months. Each time I called the investigating officer, his excuses were the same—*other commitments, pending files, lack of time.* The pattern was predictable, maddening. Deep down, I suspected **Dolion's influence was at play, pulling strings to delay and distract.** Whispers of his potential escape to Australia kept me awake at night.

Finally, after two months of fruitless waiting, I packed my bag and made the journey to Surat, determined to confront the higher authorities. My courage did not sit well with everyone. The officer in charge bristled at my directness, his irritation palpable. Yet, I held my ground. Patience is not passive—it is an act of quiet strength.

After relentless follow-ups, a personal assistant delivered the news I had longed to hear: **approval had been granted for the FIR against Dolion.** My heart surged with joy. The moment felt like a hard-won victory, proof that perseverance pays off.

The Short-Lived Victory

Armed with newfound hope, I was told to go to the concerned local police station to lodge the FIR. My hands trembled as the reader at the police station logged in, the weight of months of struggle pressing down on me. Tears of joy blurred my vision.

But some joys are fleeting, dissolving like sand through clenched fists. Within moments, the officer received a call and vanished to headquarters. Hours passed. When he finally returned, his tone was clipped, his stance rigid. *He refused to file the FIR, citing the ongoing civil suit against Dolion as the obstacle.*

I argued passionately, pointing out that the civil case had been known to all the authorities from the outset. My pleas, however, were met with a wall of indifference.

A Return to the Authorities

Deflated but not defeated, I returned to the higher authorities, demanding an explanation. Their response was disheartening—*they now insisted on a court order to proceed with the FIR.*

Their neutrality felt like betrayal. The words of Archbishop Desmond Tutu echoed in my mind:

"If you are neutral in a situation of injustice, you have chosen the side of the oppressor. If an elephant has its foot on the tail of a mouse and you say that you are neutral, the mouse will not appreciate your neutrality."

The Struggle Against Corruption

The bitter truth of corruption hung over my quest like a dark cloud. Bribery and influence are rampant, seeping into every corner of the system. While other nations battle similar demons, India's struggle feels especially acute. This venomous corruption poisons the very roots of justice.

Despite these challenges, I remain steadfast. This fight is no longer just about me—it is about the principle of standing up against wrong, about carving a path of integrity for others to follow.

In moments of doubt, I remind myself: courage is not the absence of fear but the resolve to act in spite of it. *My battle is for a better tomorrow—a legacy of resilience, strength, and unyielding hope for future generations.*

Chapter 26

A New Beginning

A Weight of Reflection

I went back to the hotel with a heavy heart, feeling utterly dejected. The events of the day had left me emotionally drained, and their weight pressed down on me like an unrelenting force. As I lay on the bed, my mind raced, replaying every moment, every word, and every decision that had led me to this point. It seemed as though humanity itself was lost, caught in a whirlwind of selfishness and disregard for the greater good. *It was as if people were abandoning their conscience as their moral compass, choosing instead to follow their own desires at the expense of everything else. I couldn't help but wonder—was anyone still afraid of* **Karma**? *Was anyone still mindful of the fact that every action, no matter how small, carries consequences?*

It's such a simple truth, yet one that seems to be forgotten by so many. While every human being is free to choose their actions, they are not free from the consequences that follow. The universe has a way of balancing the scales, even when it seems that justice has been forsaken. I thought about how quickly people could forget this fundamental truth in their pursuit of their own selfish interests, and it left me feeling disillusioned and disconnected.

The Path Ahead

By the time the first light of dawn broke through the hotel room window, I knew that clarity wouldn't come easily. The answers I sought wouldn't be revealed overnight. But I also knew that I had to keep moving forward, even in the face of uncertainty. Patience and perseverance would be my closest companions as I navigated the challenging path that lay ahead. I had to come to terms with the reality that I was in a difficult situation, one that required both endurance and determination to overcome. It wasn't something I could solve in a day or even a week, but it was something that could be managed with steady resolve. I had to accept that, in this moment, the only way out was through.

It became clear to me that, instead of dwelling on my frustrations, I needed to approach this situation with a level head. Meeting the challenges ahead with firmness and adaptability would help me better navigate the turmoil. Worrying and fuming over the circumstances would only make my burdens heavier. The more I resisted, the harder it would become. Instead, I would have to face each obstacle with a clear mind and a focused heart. This was not just a test of my patience, but of my resilience as well.

The Search for Justice

As the sun rose higher, I knew that I had to take the next step—starting over. The road to justice would not be easy, and I could not afford to waste time wallowing in despair. The first thing I needed was a competent criminal lawyer who could help me navigate the legal complexities of my situation. With a renewed sense of purpose, I began to focus on finding someone in Surat who was both capable and trustworthy.

I reached out to my senior civil lawyer, who reassured me that he would use his connections to find a criminal lawyer who was not only skilled but also honest and fair in his fees. This reassurance gave me a sense of comfort, as I had no interest in being taken advantage of during such a vulnerable time. Once again, I felt a sense of gratitude wash over me, as if an unseen hand was guiding me through the process, leading me to the right people at the right time.

Within two days, I had connected with a criminal lawyer who approached his work with the utmost sincerity and dedication. He listened intently to my concerns, asking insightful questions and offering sound advice without hesitation. It was clear that this was a man who truly cared about seeking justice, and for the first time in what felt like an eternity, I allowed myself to believe that a resolution might be possible. Together, we filed my application in the criminal court in Surat, marking the beginning of a new chapter in my fight for justice.

Embracing Life's Process

Life, I realized, is a process. It's a series of interconnected events that unfold, one after the other, and sometimes those events lead us down unexpected paths. There will be setbacks, moments of failure, and times when everything seems to be falling apart. But it's important to remember that each of these setbacks is merely part of the greater journey. Life is not a destination, but a continuous process—a process that requires us to learn, adapt, and keep moving forward, even when the way ahead is unclear.

As Richard Carlson wisely said, *"Life is a process—just one thing after another. When you lose it, just start again."* This simple yet profound truth reminded me that even in moments of despair, I always have the power to begin again. The key is to maintain a sense of hope, a belief that the future holds something better than the present. With renewed resolve and a clearer vision of what needed to be done, I prepared myself to meet the challenges ahead. I was determined to pursue justice, not just for myself, but for the greater sense of right that had been tarnished by others. *I knew that peace would not come easily, but I was willing to fight for it, step by step, no matter how long it took.*

Chapter 27

Steadfast in the Fight for Truth

The Legal Journey Begins

In the bustling city of Mumbai, my ongoing criminal case continues to unfold, progressing through the various stages of the legal process. As I mentioned in Chapter 1, the judge originally assigned to oversee my case was unexpectedly transferred to another position, and a new judge was subsequently appointed. This significant change in leadership required me to once again present my arguments and evidence in full detail to the new judge, explaining the intricacies of the case. It has been a time-consuming and challenging process, but I remain determined and resolute.

After months of patient waiting and enduring the complexities of the legal system, ***Dolion***—an individual who has been central to my case—***was finally issued summons under specific criminal sections of the law.*** This was a crucial step forward in the proceedings, as it signalled that legal action was officially being taken against him. However, despite this development, Dolion has decided to appeal the decision to the High Court, which means there will be further delays and challenges in achieving a final resolution. Although this is undoubtedly a setback, I remain confident in the fairness of the judicial system and my belief that justice is ultimately within reach. I trust that the truth will prevail, regardless of the obstacles along the way.

The Case with the Registrar of Society

In early 2023, I took another significant legal step by filing a case with the Registrar of Society. The Society, which governs the property matters of the building where my family's flats are located, had been uncooperative in providing essential documentation that my lawyer had repeatedly requested. These documents were crucial to clarifying the circumstances surrounding how my uncle's flat—purchased by my father—was transferred to Dolion. The absence of these key papers from the Society was deeply troubling, as they contained important details that would shed light on the legitimacy of the property transfer. Faced with this blatant refusal to provide the necessary documents, I had no choice but to file a formal case to seek redress for this grievance.

My father, a man of strong principles and unwavering support for his family, *had always assured me that one of the two flats in the Swaraj Housing Cooperative Society was rightfully mine. He made it clear that, should I ever face any obstacles in claiming my rightful property, I should stand firm and fight for it, knowing that he would always back me, in spirit, in my pursuit of justice.* His words of encouragement and promise of support have been a source of strength during this long and arduous battle.

The Ancestral Flat and the Civil Suit

The second flat, which was registered in my mother's name, holds special significance. It is an ancestral property that was given to her by her parents as a gift, a cherished part of her family's legacy. In my previous book, **"When He Held My Hand",** I recount the distressing events surrounding this flat, where ***Dolion used manipulative tactics to coerce my mother into signing a dubious gift deed.*** This fraudulent deed effectively transferred ownership of the flat to Dolion and his wife, Batibat. The act of deceit and coercion left my mother vulnerable and her property unjustly claimed by Dolion. In response to this, I have filed a civil suit challenging the legitimacy of the gift deed, seeking to reverse the transfer and restore my rights in my mother's flat.

The battle for my mother's ancestral flat has been particularly emotional, as it is not just a legal dispute but also a matter of family heritage. It is about protecting my mother's legacy and ensuring that Dolion's fraudulent actions are exposed and rectified in the eyes of the law. This civil suit represents my commitment to righting the wrongs that have been done and securing justice for my family.

Legal Battles in Surat and Mumbai

As I continue to write this chapter, I find myself in the midst of active civil and criminal cases against Dolion, not only in Mumbai but also in Surat. The cases in both cities mirror each other, as I pursue justice on multiple fronts. The legal battles in Surat add another layer of complexity to an already challenging situation, but they also reflect my relentless pursuit of fairness, no matter where it takes me. The process is long and fraught with anticipation, as I wait for the courts to make their decisions. Each day that passes is filled with uncertainty, but my resolve remains strong.

Perseverance and Hope

Despite the hurdles and the inevitable delays in the legal system, I remain hopeful. I hold on to the belief that justice will ultimately be served, even if it takes time. The waiting period is undoubtedly difficult, but I draw strength from the words of the great Buddhist monk Thich Nhat Hanh, who once said, *"Hope is important because it can make the present moment less difficult to bear. If we believe that tomorrow will be better, we can bear a hardship today."* These words resonate deeply with me as I continue on this journey for justice.

With hope as my guiding light, I press forward, steadfast in my belief that perseverance is key. Each step I take is a step closer to justice, and I will not rest until my family's rights are fully restored. The battle may be long, but the pursuit of justice is worth every effort. *I remain resolute, knowing that with each passing day, I am one step closer to achieving the outcome I deserve.*

Chapter 28

Unyielding Resolve: Fighting for What's Right

Ongoing Legal Struggles and Delays

As of August 2024, my ongoing case with the registrar remains unresolved, and the legal battle continues to drag on. The primary reason for this delay is the strategic tactics employed by Dolion. He often submits documents through his advocate, using these submissions as a means to intentionally postpone the proceedings. The system in Mumbai, India, is such that the registrar will not schedule the date for final arguments unless both parties have no further documents to submit. While we had already completed the submission of all relevant documents, Dolion's advocate has continuously presented new papers, offering weak excuses to justify these delays. As a result, we have been forced to file responses every time these new documents are introduced. It has become apparent that Dolion's strategy is simple: *he is trying to buy more time, likely to sell both flats in the Swaraj Housing Cooperative Society and escape to Australia.* It seems he believes in the saying *"Justice delayed is justice denied,"* but I remain hopeful and optimistic that, in the end, justice will prevail, and the truth will come to light.

A Glimmer of Hope

One day, out of the blue, the registrar issued a notice informing me of an interesting development. I was told that I could file another case with the same registrar on the same issue, but this time under a different section, namely section 154-B9. This particular section is part of the latest amendment to the Maharashtra Cooperative Societies Act, and it is known as a Suo Moto section. Essentially, this provision allows me to file a case even though I am not technically a member of the Swaraj Housing Cooperative Society, since I have witnessed and observed significant irregularities in this matter that merit legal attention.

Unlawful Property Transfer

The core issue at hand is the transfer of the flat from my paternal uncle to Dolion. To date, neither the society nor Dolion has been able to provide me, my lawyer, or the registrar with either a gift deed or a sale deed. According to the Maharashtra Cooperative Societies Act (MCSA) of 1960, all property transfers must be supported by a registered gift deed, a sale deed, or a will. However, a will is only legally valid after the death of the person transferring the property. In this case, the flat in question, was actually purchased by my father, but it was taken on my uncle's name. My uncle is still alive, so the issue of a will does not come into play here. *Without the proper legal documentation, such as a gift deed or sale deed, the transfer of the flat should be considered null and void, and the transaction should not hold any legal weight.*

A Personal Aspect

It's important to note that my intentions are not rooted in any ill will or animosity toward the Swaraj Housing Cooperative Society. I simply wish to claim my rightful share of the flat within the society. I have always believed that, even though the flat was officially registered in my father's brother's name, it would eventually pass to me. My father had made this clear to me during one of our conversations. He assured me that, should I ever find myself in a situation where I did not receive the flat—perhaps because someone might try to make an unlawful claim—I should fight for my right to it, and that he would support me in spirit, providing me with his blessings. He always understood Dolion's true nature and his propensity to manipulate situations to his advantage.

Resilience in the Face of Legal Obstacles

As I continue to navigate these complex legal challenges and uncertainties, I remain firm in my determination to honour my father's wishes. *I am resolute in my goal to secure the flat that rightfully belongs to me, no matter the obstacles or the delay tactics employed by Dolion. I will continue to fight for my rightful inheritance, and I trust that justice will eventually prevail in the end.*

Chapter 29

A Day of Betrayal and Revelation

Another shocking incident, which I have only recently become fully aware of, is the appalling attitude and atrocious behaviour displayed by Dolion, along with the heinous criminal offense he committed in relation to my father. *I have never in my life heard of any human being—especially a son—acting in such a despicable manner toward his deceased father. This betrayal has left me deeply disturbed and confused, as the very idea of such behaviour is inconceivable.*

The post-mortem of my father was conducted on February 16, 2020, a date that I will never forget. I have mentioned this traumatic event in my earlier book, but I feel the need to revisit it in more detail here. February 16, 2020, is etched in my mind not only because of the post-mortem but also because it has come to be infamously referred to as "KICK DAY." This name might seem unusual at first, but once you learn the events of this fateful day, you will understand why "KICK" is the perfect term to describe Dolion's actions.

The Day at Sterling Hospital

I distinctly remember that it was a Sunday when I went to Sterling Hospital, where my father's post-mortem was scheduled to take place. I had an intuitive feeling, a deep sense of forewarning, that Dolion would try to manipulate the forensic doctor into fabricating the post-mortem findings in his favour. I was not entirely surprised when the peon at the hospital led me to the forensic doctor's office and I saw Dolion seated across the table, attempting to charm the doctor into doing his bidding.

When I entered the room, a heavy silence hung in the air. Dolion, with a slight sneer on his face, looked at me with disdain. After a few moments, the forensic doctor, a man who had likely seen many strange occurrences in his career, instructed both Dolion and me to leave the room. He explained that he needed some time to review the documents related to my father's post-mortem. Dolion left first, throwing a final contemptuous glance at me, and I stayed seated in the chair, feeling a strange sense of foreboding.

A Moment of Truth

Once Dolion had exited the room, I requested permission from the doctor to speak with him for just two minutes. To my relief, the doctor nodded, allowing me to speak. In those precious moments, I quickly summarized the events that had led my father to the post-mortem table. The doctor listened intently, and I could see the shock and disbelief on his face as I described how my father's own son and daughter-in-law had sunk to such depths of dishonour and depravity for the sake of money. The very idea that a son would betray his father so completely seemed almost beyond comprehension.

The post-mortem report eventually came back with the somewhat ambiguous diagnosis of ***"Opinion Reserved."*** This diagnosis was inconclusive and left many questions unanswered. Months later, however, I was summoned to appear in a criminal court in Mumbai, where ***Dolion presented a letter from a doctor claiming that my father had died due to a Respiratory Tract Infection and a Urinary Tract Infection.*** This was a blatant attempt to manipulate the evidence and change the cause of death to something more acceptable. *How Dolion managed to manipulate the authorities and the reports is still a subject of speculation, but it was evident that he had orchestrated a dubious and deceptive scheme.*

The events of that day, particularly my decision to leave the hospital in the middle of the post-mortem, continue to haunt me. The choices I made, which seemed so small at the time, have left me with a deep sense of regret. I often wonder what might have been different if I had stayed and remained vigilant throughout the entire process. *Would Dolion have dared to act so boldly if I had been there to intervene?* These questions linger in my mind, and I can only hope that sharing this painful story will serve as a cautionary tale for others facing similar situations.

My Regretful Departure

In the heat of the moment, overwhelmed by emotions and the physical strain of the situation, I made the decision to inform the police officer that I needed to leave the premises. In hindsight, this decision was a grave mistake. I should have stayed and seen the process through to the end. By leaving midway, I inadvertently gave Dolion the space and opportunity to act in a manner that was both shocking and disrespectful. This was the very act that allowed him to tamper with the integrity of the post-mortem procedure, and it is something I will never forgive myself for. *It was a mistake that will forever weigh on my conscience.*

A Plea for Forgiveness

As I reflect on the events of that day, I am overwhelmed with a sense of guilt and regret. Every moment seems to replay in my mind, serving as a constant reminder of the responsibility I abandoned. I cannot help but wonder what might have been different had I stayed. *Would Dolion have dared to act with such audacity if I had been there to witness and confront his actions?* I can only plead for my father's forgiveness, though I know that my remorse cannot undo the damage that was done. I hope that by sharing this story, others might learn from my mistake and stay vigilant in moments that truly matter, especially when justice is on the line.

The Unthinkable Act

After the post-mortem was completed, Dolion was entrusted with my father's organs. He was supposed to transport them safely to the police station, where they would be stored before being sent to the Pathology Lab for further forensic analysis. This is a standard procedure following a post-mortem. At first, Dolion was reluctant to take the organs in his hands. *While I knew that Dolion had a deep hatred for my father, I had no idea just how far that hatred went.* Despite his obvious aversion, Dolion was eventually forced by the police officer to hold the organs, (my father's spleen, liver, and brain). He took them with a look of disgust on his face.

What happened next was beyond comprehension. Dolion, in a final act of spite, placed the organs on the floorboard of his chauffeur-driven car and—this is the part that still sickens me—**he actually placed his foot on them.** The police officer, no doubt aware of the egregious nature of this act, reminded him that what he was doing was deeply disrespectful. Dolion, however, didn't seem to care. He lifted his foot, only to once again stamp it down on the organs, as though he was sending a clear message to the world that he had no respect whatsoever for his father, even in death.

This act, this unthinkable display of contempt, is something that no one should ever have to witness. I am certain that no one has ever heard of a son treating his father in such a despicable manner. In most cultures, even when a person is deceased, respect is shown, and the remains are treated with dignity. The ashes of a loved one are carried with reverence, not tossed aside or disrespected in such a brutal way. *But, as I have repeatedly said, Dolion is not even fit to be called a human being.*

Further Manipulation of Evidence

In addition to his appalling actions with my father's organs, **Dolion further manipulated the authorities by ensuring that the specimens of my father's organs were sent without any identification labels.** This was a clear attempt to undermine the forensic process. The organs, which were supposed to be critical evidence in the investigation, were simply left in a cupboard, unidentified and neglected. It is highly questionable what, if anything, was actually sent for forensic analysis. *Without proper identification, the integrity of the post-mortem was compromised, and it is no wonder that the results were inconclusive and unhelpful.*

A Lesson Learned

Looking back on these events, I have learned a painful but valuable lesson. In moments of crisis, when the integrity of justice and truth is on the line, it is crucial to stay present and see things through to the end. While I cannot change the past, I hope that by sharing this experience, I can help others avoid the same mistakes I made. The events of that day have shaken me to my core, but they have also taught me the importance of vigilance, of never allowing manipulation and deceit to go unchecked.

The Unravelling Truth

Dolion's manipulation of the authorities was both clever and disturbing. By ensuring that the organs were sent without proper identification, he compromised the entire forensic process. The specimen that was supposed to shed light on my father's cause of death was rendered useless, casting serious doubts on the findings of the post-mortem examination. Given these circumstances, it is no surprise that the final diagnosis was inconclusive. *It was as if the entire process was designed to protect Dolion, not uncover the truth.*

The Illusion of Justice

Dolion's actions, however, do not go unnoticed. While he may have successfully manipulated the post-mortem process for his own ends, he should not be so confident in his ability to evade justice forever. What he and Batibat did to my father may escape human justice, but they cannot escape the Ultimate Judgment. The Supreme Power will hold them accountable for their actions.

The Awaited Reckoning

As I write these words, there is a sense of anticipation building within me. I wait, with bated breath, for the truth to eventually unravel. While human systems may fail and justice may be delayed, the Supreme Power will not be deceived. ***The Day of Reckoning will come, and when it does, Dolion and those who helped him in his deceitful actions will have to answer for their wrongdoings***. Truth and justice will prevail in the end, and the reckoning for all those involved will be inevitable.

Chapter 30

Disrespect the Dead

In many cultures, societies, and legal systems around the world, the treatment of the deceased holds immense significance. The way in which the dead are treated is often a reflection of cultural values, respect for the individual's life, and the dignity of human existence. *This chapter explores the concept of respecting the dead, examining both the legal frameworks designed to protect their remains and the ethical considerations that arise when dealing with the deceased.*

Forms of Desecration

Desecration of a deceased individual refers to actions that violate the sanctity or integrity of their remains, which can take many forms. These acts of desecration can be deeply harmful, not only to the individual whose body is disrespected but also to their family, community, and society at large. Desecration can manifest in numerous ways, including, but not limited to:

1) *Mixing the remains of the deceased:*

Desecration can involve the inappropriate mixing of ashes, bones, or other remains without consent from the deceased's family or legal representatives. This act can be particularly egregious, as it undermines the identity and individuality of the person who has passed away. The mixing of remains may be viewed as an act of disrespect to the deceased's memory, potentially disrupting their final resting place and desecrating the sanctity of their burial or cremation rites. Such actions are not only legally questionable but also ethically problematic.

2) *Treating the deceased's remains in a disrespectful manner:*

Another form of desecration includes the mishandling, improper display, or neglect of the deceased's remains. Physical acts such as disturbing the body, improperly storing or displaying the remains, or leaving them in unsuitable conditions can be seen as gross violations of both societal norms and ethical standards. These acts may cause emotional distress to the deceased's family members, who are entitled to mourn and remember their loved one with dignity. Inappropriate actions may range from careless treatment to deliberate acts of violence or destruction, all of which cause harm to the memory and respect due to the dead.

Rights of the Dead in India

In the legal context, many countries have specific laws in place to protect the remains of the deceased, and India is no exception. ***In Indian legal practice, respect for the deceased is enshrined in the law as a fundamental principle. Section 297 of the Indian Penal Code (IPC) clearly outlines that if any individual offers any form of indignity to a human corpse, they shall be subject to punishment.*** The punishment may include imprisonment for a term that can extend up to one year, or a fine, or both, depending on the severity of the act. This provision underscores the importance placed on treating human remains with dignity and respect, highlighting that even in death, individuals are entitled to protection under the law.

Additionally, the Supreme Court of India has consistently reinforced this notion of dignity and respect for the deceased through various landmark judgments. In significant rulings, such as the case of Union of India vs. The deceased's family members, the Court emphasized that the Right to Life, Fair Treatment, and Dignity under Article 21 of the Indian Constitution are not restricted solely to the living but extend to the deceased as well. This interpretation of the law signals a broader understanding of human rights, asserting that dignity persists beyond death, and human remains deserve protection and respectful treatment after an individual has passed away. This principle was further extended in the "**Akshray Adhikar Abhiyan**" case, where the Court upheld that these rights, particularly the right to dignity, are enduring and extend even after death, ensuring that the dead are treated with the same respect afforded to the living.

International Perspective: United Nations Commission on Human Rights

On the global stage, the United Nations Commission on Human Rights has also taken a stance on the treatment of human remains, acknowledging the inherent dignity of individuals, even after their death. *The 2005 United Nations resolution on human rights and forensic science addressed the need for proper management, handling, and disposal of human remains, emphasizing that such practices must align with principles of dignity and respect for the deceased.* This resolution asserted that the right to dignity does not cease upon death, but instead extends beyond the grave. The United Nations recognized that human rights should encompass the treatment of individuals even after they have passed, and this idea resonates with similar principles upheld in domestic laws across various countries.

The United Nations' stance on human dignity aligns closely with the views expressed by the Supreme Court of India. In both cases, there is a clear recognition that the deceased should be treated with respect, and that dignity does not end with life. This shared perspective emphasizes the importance of upholding the rights of the dead, demonstrating a universal commitment to honouring human dignity, whether in life or after death. These international standards provide a foundation for the ethical treatment of human remains, reinforcing the idea that the sanctity of the human body and the memory of the deceased must be preserved with the utmost respect and care.

In conclusion, both domestic and international legal frameworks recognize the importance of treating the deceased with dignity and respect. The ethical considerations surrounding the treatment of the dead reflect deeply ingrained societal values, emphasizing the need to protect the deceased from harm and desecration. *As we continue to evolve as a global society, these principles of respect for the dead should remain a cornerstone of both law and ethical practice, ensuring that all individuals, living or deceased, are treated with the dignity they deserve.*

Chapter 31

Unveiling the Shadows of the Past

A Glimpse into the Past

The Prelude: Life in 1976

As I take a nostalgic walk down memory lane, I find myself reflecting on two significant incidents that serve to further expose the dark, hidden side of Dolion. *These incidents, which occurred long ago, have stayed with me, constantly reminding me of the troubling nature of his character.* It was in the year 1976, a time that feels like a lifetime ago now. At that time, I was studying science at Jai Hind College, trying to focus on my academics and future. My father had purchased a Padmini Fiat car in 1973. At that point, it was a source of pride and convenience for our family. While I would diligently take the bus to college every day, Dolion, who always sought ways to make an impression, would drive the car, symbolizing his need to assert dominance over ordinary life. I have already discussed in great detail the issue of gender discrimination in my previous book, which added further layers to this situation.

One evening, in the middle of that year, Dolion had indulged in a few drinks (as usual, they were consumed outside the home—drinking in the house was strictly forbidden during those days). Our parents, especially my father, were known to be very strict about such matters. Alcohol was seen as an absolute no-no in our house. My father, being a doctor, upheld this principle with particular seriousness. In those days, Dolion never drank at home, but I'm sure it was a different story when he was outside. Fast forward to the present day, and Dolion drinks freely in the house, without a second thought. Sometimes, I can't help but wonder if his drinking habits are linked to his inability to find peaceful sleep. After everything he has done and the guilt he has accumulated, there's no way he could be getting a restful, normal sleep. His wife, I assume, must rely on antidepressants or sleeping pills to get the rest she needs. I am certain that at one point in her life, she was indeed on antidepressants, which only adds another layer of complexity to this troubled household.

The Night of Recklessness

The defining incident took place one evening when Dolion, in a state of intoxication, was behind the wheel of my father's car. It was in Andheri, and he was speeding down the highway with no concern for the rules or the safety of others. *In his drunken state, he lost control and knocked down a traffic cop.* The incidence itself was a minor consequence in his mind. What was worse was the fact that Dolion didn't even bother to check on the condition of the cop or to stop and assess the situation. Instead, he decided to flee the scene in the belief that he was somehow clever and would evade responsibility. His arrogance led him to think that his actions would go unnoticed, but he underestimated the police. If you harm a cop, there's little chance of escaping the consequences. Another officer had observed the scene, and the car's license plate had been noted. Later that very same day, the policeman showed up at our residence.

It was a typical evening in our household. My father, dressed in his customary white attire, was sitting in the dispensary, busy consulting his patients. The front room of our flat had been converted into a clinic, and the space was filled with the usual hum of daily life. Dolion, trying to keep the entire incident quiet, had slipped into his room without saying a word to anyone. He didn't inform my father or any of us about what had happened. He hoped that his actions would go unnoticed. However, his hopes were dashed when the officer entered the dispensary. My father, startled and caught off guard, could not believe what he was hearing. The angry police officer recounted the entire incident in a tone full of frustration. My father, who was known for his calm and composed demeanour, was speechless. The officer informed him that Dolion was being charged with attempted murder for running over the traffic cop.

A Father's Desperate Plea

What followed was a scene of utter desperation. My father, deeply concerned and shocked by the severity of the situation, fell to his knees and pleaded with the officer, hands folded in a gesture of utmost humility. He even went so far as to touch the officer's feet, tears streaming down his face as he begged for mercy. ***It was a heartbreaking moment for me to witness, as my father, a man of principle and dignity, was brought to his knees by the consequences of his son's actions.*** The officer, observing my father's emotional plea and recognizing the good reputation he had in the community, finally agreed not to arrest Dolion on the spot. However, the officer issued a stern warning: my father needed to be aware of Dolion's dangerous tendencies and should take immediate action to correct his behaviour. The officer even stated that if Dolion's reckless behaviour wasn't curbed, it was likely that one day he would end up a criminal. How prophetic those words were! In hindsight, my father should have been far stricter with Dolion at that point. He should have taken firm action and punished him for what he had done. At the time of the incident, Dolion must have been about 20 or 22 years old.

A Moment of Missed Discipline

It is often said that if you turn a blind eye to the misdeeds of your child when they are young, the consequences will only escalate. Slowly, like a creeping darkness, the Devil within them starts to emerge, and one day, as a parent, you are left wondering where you went wrong in your efforts to raise them. My father, despite his best intentions, made the mistake of not being strict enough with Dolion when it mattered most. This moment of leniency would come to haunt us all.

The Consequences of Neglect

It's crucial to remember that punishment is not meant for revenge or to satisfy a thirst for justice, but rather, it is intended to reduce crime and to reform those who are caught in its grasp. My father, despite everything, never could bring himself to punish Dolion in any meaningful way. To this day, my father's car remains in Dolion's possession. Out of fear—fear that the legal consequences of his past crime could resurface at any moment—Dolion has taken measures to hide his tracks. He has changed the car's license plate, perhaps thinking that this small act will help him evade responsibility for his past actions. Yet, deep down, I believe that **"Karma is Justice"**. It doesn't matter where we hide or how deeply we try to bury the truth; it always finds a way to surface. No matter how much we attempt to escape the consequences, the truth will eventually come to light, and accountability will follow.

The shadows of the past may seem far away, but they never remain hidden forever.

Chapter 32

The Unchecked Legacy

The Long -Term Consequences of Neglect

The words of the cop that day were now proving to be undeniably true. My father had failed to address the growing evil within Dolion when it was still in its infancy. His extreme fondness for his son, Dolion, coupled with his indulgent attitude, allowed a dangerous and destructive pattern to take root, one that only grew worse with time. If my father had taken strict, decisive action when Dolion was still just a young man of 20, I have no doubt that Dolion would not have had the audacity or the courage to commit the reckless and malicious acts that he did in 2012, a staggering 32 years later. The absence of accountability in Dolion's formative years had allowed his behaviour to spiral unchecked, leading to the chain of events that followed.

The Incident at the Hospital

It all started with a distant relative of ours, a man who had, unfortunately, found himself on the wrong side of the law. His transgressions were compounded by a series of severe health issues, which led to his hospitalization in a government-run medical facility. However, despite his hospitalization, he was still kept under strict surveillance, confined to a special section of the hospital designated as the hospital jail. This particular facility had very strict visitation policies. Only family members who had obtained prior approval were allowed to visit him, making it almost impossible for anyone to visit without proper clearance. However, Dolion, who had always believed himself to be above the law—and continues to do so to this day—decided to take matters into his own hands, bypassing the system entirely.

In an act of audacity and complete disregard for the rules, Dolion decided to disguise himself as a doctor. He donned a doctor's coat and draped a stethoscope around his neck, fully intending to visit our relative under the false pretence of being a medical professional. His reasoning, so he thought, was simple: his disguise would surely be enough to fool the hospital staff and, more importantly, the police officers stationed at the facility. Dolion's belief was that no one would question a doctor, especially one in full medical garb, and that he could easily pass himself off as the officially appointed doctor for the inmates.

The Confrontation

Dolion's plan seemed to work at first. He successfully made his way through the first two steel barricades that separated him from the restricted part of the hospital. Each time he passed through a checkpoint, his confidence grew, and he felt as though he were outsmarting everyone around him. However, his good fortune began to run out when he reached the third barricade. The cop on duty at that post, a diligent and honest officer, did his job without hesitation. He was no fool, and he was not about to let someone bypass the system simply because they wore a doctor's coat.

The officer asked Dolion to provide his credentials, a simple and straightforward request that Dolion could not fulfil. In that moment, Dolion's façade began to crumble. Despite his insistence that he was indeed a doctor, the officer, following protocol, demanded a written letter of permission from the hospital authorities. Dolion, however, had no such letter, nor any valid explanation for why he was there without it.

At that moment, Dolion realized the severity of the situation. This was no longer just a harmless ruse. The cop's sharp questioning and his unwavering stance left Dolion exposed and vulnerable. The fear that he had long avoided now gripped him. He understood that the officer could easily call for backup, and he would find himself facing charges for impersonating a doctor and attempting to breach security. The realization hit him like a cold wave—he was moments away from being arrested once again.

A Narrow Escape

As fate would have it, or perhaps as a result of some good karma from a past life, Dolion somehow managed to escape with minimal consequences. The cop, though firm in his questioning and clearly aware that Dolion was trying to deceive him, chose to act with surprising leniency. Instead of escalating the matter, he made a note of the incident in his notebook, recorded the details, and issued Dolion a warning. The cop allowed him to leave, giving Dolion a rare and unexpected chance to walk away unscathed.

This moment of mercy, however, did little to humble Dolion. Instead, he took it as yet another victory, one that he would continue to boast about in the years that followed. To this day, he tells the story of how he managed to cross the hospital's barricades, how he supposedly outsmarted the law by using his acting skills and his quick thinking. He relishes in the praise and admiration of his ability to deceive others, but conveniently omits the part where he was terrified when he realized that his ruse had been uncovered. He doesn't acknowledge the sheer panic he felt in the face of imminent arrest. For him, it was always about the glory of his success, never the fear of his failure.

The truth, however, is that Dolion's actions were not heroic or impressive. Rather, they were a reflection of his unchecked narcissism. Dolion is, and always has been, a covert narcissist. His actions, which continue to be indulged and overlooked, have had far-reaching consequences. The ripples from this particular incident, just like so many others, continue to affect our lives. *The story of his arrogance and his brazen disregard for the law is a testament to the dangers of failing to address harmful behaviour when it first rears its head. His legacy, unchecked and unchallenged, has only grown worse with time, leaving behind a trail of broken trust and fractured relationships.*

Chapter 33

The Courtroom Revelation

National Women's Day

On the 9th of August 2024, a day celebrated annually as National Women's Day, a moment of great significance unfolded in the Surat Court, one that would forever reaffirm the wisdom of the age-old adage: *"What is done in the dark will come to light."* This day was not only marked by the commemoration of the countless achievements of women, but also by an unexpected unmasking of deceit, betrayal, and truth. *What had been concealed for so long in the shadows was finally brought into the glaring light of justice.*

As I prepared for the hearing, Karla Grimes' words rang clear in my mind: *"A Narcissist paints a picture of himself as being a victim or innocent in all aspects. They will be offended by the truth. But what is done in the dark will come to light. Time has a way of showing people's true colours."* These words struck a deep chord with me as I stood on the brink of what could be a pivotal moment in my life. The case, which I had long awaited, centered around the civil dispute over my grandfather's bungalow, a piece of property that had long been a symbol of our family legacy. It was in this courtroom that everything—truth, betrayal, manipulation—would come to a head.

The Courtroom Drama

On this fateful day, Dolion, who had never once attended any of the hearings in person before, made his first appearance in the Surat court. In all previous sessions, only his lawyers had been present to represent him, painting a picture of a man perpetually on the move—an endlessly busy medical professional, supposedly too occupied with his demanding work to be physically present in court. But on this day, he appeared, and his very presence seemed to signal an escalation in the drama. The case had always centered on the ancestral property, the bungalow that my late grandfather had so clearly handed down to my father in his will. This matter has been discussed in great detail back in the earlier chapters, where I described how Dolion, in a move of staggering audacity, had sold the bungalow for a huge sum—1 Crore Rupees—without ever revealing the full truth to me, his own family.

For months, Dolion had downplayed the value of the bungalow, claiming he had sold it for only 50 lakh Rupees, a figure that seemed suspiciously low given the prime location and size of the property. Despite the repeated encouragement from the Civil Court Judge to reach an amicable settlement and resolve the matter outside of court,

Dolion had consistently offered me a mere 25 lakh Rupees, dismissing the value of the bungalow and attempting to position himself as a magnanimous benefactor, doing me a great favour by offering that amount. He made it clear that his condition for this paltry sum was that I drop all legal cases against him, both civil and criminal, which were ongoing in the courts of Mumbai and Surat. This offer, to him, was a generous one, but to me, it was a mere attempt to escape the consequences of his own dishonest actions.

My response was immediate and resolute. I refused to accept his offer, and in return, I made a counter-proposal: I would pay him 25 lakh Rupees, but only if he agreed to return the bungalow to me, where it rightfully belonged. My proposal was a fair one, an attempt to right the wrongs that had been done, to restore what had been stolen from us by deceit.

The Unveiling of Deception

It was during this hearing that the truth, hidden for so long beneath layers of falsehoods and fabrications, was finally brought to light. The revelation that Dolion had not sold the bungalow for the 50 lakh Rupees he had claimed, but for a staggering 1 Crore Rupees, sent shockwaves through the courtroom. It was a classic case of deception—*Dolion had hoped to pull the wool over my eyes, to keep the full amount of the sale concealed in order to benefit from the under-the-table dealings that are sadly all too common in real estate transactions in India.* The practice of hiding the full sale price to avoid paying taxes was something that most people in the business knew well, and Dolion had clearly hoped to exploit this loophole to his advantage.

His plan was simple: if he could maintain the façade of a modest sale price, I would never know the true value of the bungalow, and he would be able to keep the difference. But in the courtroom, with the evidence laid bare before all, Dolion's strategy crumbled like a house of cards. His lies, which had once seemed so expertly crafted, fell apart under the scrutiny of the law. It was no longer a matter of his word against mine—it was a case of cold, hard facts.

Conclusion

The hearing on National Women's Day, a day that was meant to honour the accomplishments and contributions of women everywhere, turned out to be far more than just a celebration. It became a powerful reminder of the enduring strength of truth and justice. Dolion's carefully constructed façade shattered in that courtroom, and his attempt to manipulate and deceive was exposed for all to see.

As I left the courtroom, the words of Karla Grimes reverberated in my mind, stronger than ever before. The truth, it seemed, had finally emerged, just as she had predicted. Time had indeed revealed Dolion's true colours, and it was clear for all to see what kind of man he was.

The events of that day underscored the importance of perseverance in the pursuit of justice, and the necessity of standing firm in the face of dishonesty and manipulation. In the end, the truth had triumphed, and Dolion's deceitful schemes had been laid bare for all to witness.

That day served as a powerful reminder to me, and to everyone involved, that the pursuit of justice requires unwavering resolve. No matter how dark the shadows of deceit may seem, the light of truth will always find its way through. *In the end, the truth will shine brightly, dispelling all lies, and no one can hide from it forever.*

Chapter 34

Dolion the Actor

The First Appearance in Surat Civil Court

On the 9th of August 2024, a Friday, Dolion made his highly anticipated first appearance in the Surat Civil Court. His entrance was nothing short of a performance, an act that seemed almost theatrical in nature. He walked slowly, almost as if he were exhausted from an invisible burden, each step dragging behind him as though his body could no longer bear the weight of the world. His face, completely concealed by a large mask, gave no hint of his true emotions, adding an air of mystery to his already dramatic persona. His shoes, in an alarming state of disrepair, were tattered and barely held together. Two of his toes could be seen peeking out from the holes in the torn fabric. The shoes bore cuts and slashes, which seemed deliberately inflicted with the sharp edge of a knife, making it clear that their condition was the result of intentional neglect. His pants, which hung loosely around his waist, were frayed at the edges, hemmed with an assortment of threads in various colours. Some of these threads had come loose entirely, leaving the hemline hanging down awkwardly in a display of disarray. His shirt, once a modest beige, had become faded and stained in places, showing clear signs of wear and tear. It was dirty, torn in several places, and looked as though it had been through countless hardships. *The overall image he projected was that of a destitute beggar, someone seemingly without the means to afford even the most basic of clothing.*

The Courtroom Drama

When Dolion addressed the court, his voice was weak and faint, as though speaking took an immense amount of effort. He claimed to be exhausted, having worked 16 to 17 hours a day, painting a picture of someone labouring tirelessly in an attempt to make ends meet. However, the judge, unimpressed by his dramatic display, calmly requested that he remove his mask to allow for better clarity. She asked him to explain his financial situation, pointing out that with such long working hours, he should have accumulated a substantial fortune by now. The judge, with a sceptical tone, questioned Dolion about his reasons for contesting a share of the family's ancestral home. Despite her pressing inquiry, Dolion could not offer a satisfactory response, leaving the court in a tense silence.

Attempting to deflect the judge's scrutiny, Dolion resorted to attempting to malign me. However, the judge quickly intervened, reminding him that the matter at hand was not about personal attacks but about property, and such irrelevant matters had no place in the current proceedings.

Negotiations and Legal Manoeuvres

The judge, keen to resolve the matter, offered Dolion another opportunity to present his terms for negotiation. However, Dolion remained stubborn and stood by his initial offer, which was immediately met with a strong and robust argument from my lawyer. My lawyer, with great precision, laid out the terms for resolving the case. *For the settlement to proceed, Dolion was required to provide a flat in the Swaraj Housing Cooperative Society, or its equivalent in the current market value, which was estimated to be around 7 crores. Additionally, Dolion was expected to offer half of the market value of the grandfather's shares, which amounted to approximately 5 crores, along with a sum of 50 lakhs for the Surat Bungalow.* My lawyer made it clear that even a slightly lower offer would be considered, assuring the judge of his ability to persuade me to accept a reasonable settlement.

Dolion, upon hearing these terms, was visibly taken aback by how well-informed my Surat lawyer was about matters in Mumbai. This display of knowledge unsettled him, as Dolion, a covert narcissist, typically kept his team of lawyers in the dark, only sharing selective and strategic information. This was part of his calculated effort to maintain control over the legal proceedings and to prevent any advice that might work against his own self-interests.

The Judge's Wisdom

The civil judge in Surat, perceptive and sharp as ever, quickly saw through Dolion's manipulative tactics. She was aware of his deceptive nature and understood that he was attempting to play a game, likely in the hopes of wearing down the opposition. Despite this, the judge displayed a remarkable sense of fairness. Recognizing that Dolion's behaviour was more about evasion than negotiation, she granted him a short adjournment, giving him one final chance to reconsider his position. However, when Dolion returned, he remained unwavering in his stance, offering only a mere 25 lakh rupees. This amount was so far below what had been proposed that it left no room for further negotiation, and as a result, the civil case was set to continue.

Attempted Bribery

On the same day, ***Dolion, apparently desperate to secure a favourable outcome, made an attempt to bribe my junior lawyer.*** He cleverly avoided approaching the senior lawyer, who, at 82 years old, exuded a stern, no-nonsense presence. Dolion, calculating that he could easily influence the younger, seemingly more impressionable lawyer, Kanha, sought to exploit his position. ***However, Kanha, who was both principled and deeply rooted in his faith, was not swayed by Dolion's advances.*** With calm resolve, he informed Dolion that our team was committed to fighting the case within the bounds of the law, and no amount of external influence would change that fact.

Despite Dolion's dramatic portrayal of financial ruin and hardship, Kanha remained firm in his conviction. He pointed out the glaring contradiction in Dolion's claims of poverty, noting how frequently he and his wife travelled between Mumbai and Australia. This travel, which was frequent and lavish, was proof enough that Dolion's assertions of financial struggle were, in fact, far from the truth. *Kanha, with a quiet confidence, reminded Dolion that even if he managed to evade justice in the court of law, he would ultimately face accountability in the Highest Court of all—the Ultimate Court of Justice.* Dolion, who had hoped to manipulate the legal process in his favour, was left with no viable escape.

Chapter 35

Understanding the Narcissist's Aversion to "No"

The Narcissist's Need for Control

"Narcissists dislike the word 'no' because it represents a direct challenge to their perceived authority and control," explains Dr. McGeehan. For a narcissist, hearing "no" can feel like a deep personal rejection or a denial of their significance, posing a serious threat to their fragile ego. This strong aversion is rooted in their overwhelming need for constant external validation and the relentless desire for others to agree with them in order to sustain their inflated self-worth. When they are confronted with "no," they may feel like they are being diminished or negated, which directly conflicts with their idealized sense of self.

Narcissists are often unable to process disagreement in a healthy way because they have been conditioned to expect admiration and compliance from others. Any refusal can trigger intense feelings of insecurity or inadequacy, which they may try to hide through manipulation, anger, or even further demands for compliance. The aversion to "no" becomes a reflection of their deep-seated fear of being exposed as less than perfect or in control. The struggle to accept "no" can become a defining characteristic of their relationships, as they perceive any form of boundary-setting as a personal attack on their authority and superiority.

The Impact of Criticism

In addition to challenging their control, the word "no" symbolizes a form of criticism that strikes at the very core of a narcissist's sense of self. *"This criticism cuts deeply for a narcissist, who must always be seen as superior,"* says Dr. Michelle Goldman, PhD, a well-respected psychologist and Media Advisor for the Hope for Depression Research Foundation. To a narcissist, any form of disagreement or boundary-setting is experienced as a direct assault on their perceived superiority and their carefully constructed image of perfection. The narcissist's intense need for validation means that even mild criticism can feel like a catastrophic event, triggering feelings of humiliation or anger.

This overwhelming sensitivity to criticism stems from their fragile self-esteem, which, rather than being solid and stable, is precariously reliant on the approval of others. For a narcissist, being told "no" is not just a simple refusal; it becomes an existential challenge to their sense of worth and identity. This response to criticism can create tension and conflict in relationships, as the narcissist may react defensively or aggressively to defend their fragile ego. The inability to accept even the smallest amount of critique can hinder personal growth and prevent them from developing the emotional resilience necessary for healthy interpersonal dynamics.

Dolion's Struggle with Boundaries

For Dolion, a self-identified narcissist, the word "no" becomes more than just a refusal; it marks a boundary that he finds almost impossible to accept. *Dolion firmly believes that he knows best and that his decisions should automatically dictate how things should unfold.* He perceives the word "no" as a threat to his authority and power, which he holds dear. However, Dolion must eventually come to terms with the fact that there are some things in life that cannot be controlled or bought with wealth, such as basic manners, personal integrity, and moral values. Recognizing these inherent values is crucial for personal growth and the ability to form healthier, more balanced relationships.

Despite his resistance to boundaries, Dolion faces a reality that even he cannot escape: the world does not revolve around his desires or expectations. The refusal of others to comply with his wishes is a natural part of life, and learning to accept it is essential for his emotional well-being. For Dolion, the challenge lies not only in accepting "no" but in understanding that respect for others' autonomy and boundaries is a key component of meaningful and lasting relationships.

A Note of Gratitude

As I reflect on the journey thus far, I want to take a moment to extend my heartfelt gratitude to my attorneys. Your unwavering dedication, tireless work ethic, and commitment to ensuring our success have made all the difference. Throughout the years, your expertise and guidance have been invaluable, and I am deeply appreciative of your continued support. While it is your job to represent and advise, for me, it is far more personal. Your efforts have been integral to the progress we've made, and I will always be thankful for how you have consistently gone above and beyond in every way possible. Your professionalism, attention to detail, and unflagging support have not gone unnoticed, and I am sincerely grateful for everything you have done to help make our journey smoother and more successful. Thank you for being such an important part of this chapter in my life.

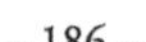

Chapter 36

A Journey to Lapland

Today is September 24, 2024, and my mind is flooded with vivid and beautiful memories of Lapland, a magical place I had the opportunity to visit five years ago. In September 2019, I set off on a solo journey to this enchanting land located above the Arctic Circle in the Scandinavian countries. It was a once-in-a-lifetime experience that I will forever cherish, and to this day, it remains my favourite international destination. For this adventure, I meticulously crafted my own itinerary for 21 days, fully embracing the freedom and self-discovery that come with traveling alone.

My plan was to fly from Mumbai to Stockholm, and then return home from Copenhagen to Mumbai, a well-thought-out route that allowed me to experience the best of Scandinavia.

Discovering the Hidden Gems

The first step in my planning process was to mark destinations on a hand-drawn map of the Scandinavian countries, a map that would soon serve as a guide for my journey. Google became an invaluable tool, helping me discover off-the-beaten-path locations that I had never heard of before. One such place was Kiruna, a town located far to the north of the Arctic Circle in Sweden. To my surprise, I realized that Kiruna was the same town I had seen years ago on the National Geographic Channel, where it was featured for its unique situation: houses were being relocated because the expanding coal mines were causing the area to submerge. The government had given residents three options: accept compensation and leave, move to alternative accommodations, or have their homes physically relocated, a decision that mainly applied to churches and heritage buildings. During my visit, I even witnessed a house being lifted and placed onto a giant crane trolley to be moved to a safer location.

The Enchanting Ice Hotel

Among the many wonders of Kiruna, one of the most unforgettable was the 365 Ice Hotel. Originally, the hotel was constructed only for the winter months, melting away every summer, but since 2014, it has remained open year-round. When I visited in 2019, staying in the hotel cost approximately 16,000 INR per night. However, tourists could enter and explore the hotel for a nominal fee of 4,000 INR, which was a reasonable price to experience this extraordinary creation. I made sure to visit the hotel when it opened to the public at 11:00 a.m. every morning. The owners of Camp Alta, where I was staying, kindly offered me morning drop-offs and evening pick-ups at my chosen destinations, making my travels incredibly convenient.

At the Ice Hotel entrance, guests were provided with thick, warm coats and gumboots to help combat the chill. Each room within the hotel featured unique and intricate ice designs—ice beds, ice staircases, and ice glasses—each room more mesmerizing than the last. One room that particularly stood out was the *"mermaid room,"* where the ice bed was surrounded by beautiful, sculpted mermaids, creating an ethereal atmosphere that I will never forget.

Santa Claus Village in Rovaniemi

While planning my journey, I also stumbled upon Santa Claus Village in Rovaniemi, Finland, which is located right on the Arctic Circle. As a child growing up in a convent school, I had always believed in Santa Claus and the idea that he resided somewhere in the north. Friends used to send letters to him, though none of us knew exactly where they went. Visiting the Santa Claus Village in Rovaniemi felt like stepping into a dream. I had the opportunity to visit the Santa Claus post office, where letters from all over the world, including India, were neatly stacked and organized on labelled shelves, awaiting a response from Santa.

But the true highlight of this experience was meeting Santa Claus himself. Outside his chamber, a young girl asked me where I was from, and I proudly shared that

I was from India. When I finally entered the chamber, Santa greeted me with a warm "Namaste, Namaste," and we spent about five delightful minutes chatting. I even received videos and pictures of our interaction for a small fee, preserving the magic of that moment. Visiting Santa in September was truly a blessing. Later, I read stories of families from all over the world who visited Rovaniemi with their children in December, hoping to meet Santa. Unfortunately, during the busy holiday season, Santa had very little time to interact with each child. Many parents were disappointed, as they had spent their entire year's savings to make their children's Christmas dreams come true. The experience had become more of a rushed photo opportunity than the magical encounter they had imagined.

The Majestic Northern Lights

As my journey continued, I encountered many more amazing experiences, but two memories in particular stand out: Kiruna and Rovaniemi. One of the most awe-inspiring moments of my trip was witnessing the Northern Lights in Rovaniemi. At the time, this stunning natural phenomenon was unfamiliar to most of my friends, patients, and relatives, who had never seen it or even heard of it. But now, in 2024, the world has become much more aware of this extraordinary spectacle, and even people in India are familiar with its beauty.

I often remind my friends that we don't travel to escape life, but rather to ensure that life doesn't escape us. Sometimes, travel leaves us speechless, only to later turn us into storytellers, eager to share the magic we've experienced. My journey to Lapland was one such experience—one that I will cherish forever and one that continues to inspire me to seek out new adventures around the world.

Chapter 37

Reflections and Connections

A Startling Incident

A few days ago, as I was casually flipping through the newspaper, I happened upon an article that immediately caught my attention. It detailed an unusual and somewhat startling incident in which an empty tanker truck, for reasons that were unclear, overturned and crashed through the wall of a small, dilapidated bungalow in the early hours of the morning. This particular bungalow, located near a busy traffic signal in the bustling, vibrant suburb of Bandra in Mumbai, immediately piqued my interest. There were several reasons, both personal and contextual, that made this story stand out to me.

The article described how the tanker had been speeding at the time of the accident, and as it approached the signal, a jeep coming from the opposite direction collided with it. It was a fortunate turn of events that neither the driver of the jeep nor the driver of the tanker was seriously injured in the incident, which, on the surface, seemed like a bizarre and near-fatal accident. As I continued reading, I encountered a detail that caught me completely off guard—the bungalow in question belonged to none other than Roshni, an old school friend of mine. *The realization struck me like a bolt from the blue, flooding me with a rush of emotions—nostalgia, concern, and disbelief.*

A Personal Connection

I had known Roshni for many years, and the thought of her bungalow being involved in such an alarming accident left me deeply unsettled. What struck me even more was the fact that this bungalow had been the subject of interest for several builders eager to purchase the property due to its prime location. The bungalow had, over the years, become a symbol of potential development. The only person residing in the aging structure was Roshni's elderly brother, who had been struggling with various health issues.

After reading the article, I felt a deep sense of urgency and concern for my friend and her family. Without wasting a moment, I picked up the phone and called Roshni. She confirmed the details of the incident and shared her suspicion that the crash was not an accident at all but rather a deliberate act, possibly orchestrated to intimidate her brother into selling the property. The most fortunate aspect of the whole situation was that the wall of the house had held up and was still intact, sparing them from more serious damage. Roshni and her brother are currently the sole owners of the bungalow. Although Roshni lives some distance away in her marital home, she frequently visits the bungalow to care for her ailing brother, showing her unwavering commitment to her family.

The Bond of Friendship

Roshni and I have been friends for as long as I can remember—since our nursery school days. Looking back on our shared memories, I realize how precious those early moments of friendship were. One memory that stands out to me clearly is from the day I first entered Convent School. On that first day, my paternal uncle had accompanied me, which, at the time, made me feel both nervous and reassured.

My uncle, who was not well-educated and had no stable source of income, had found a temporary refuge with our family. He did not even own a house and relied on my father for shelter. Despite his circumstances, my father, in his ever-generous way, provided my uncle with a home, a job, and financial support, never once making him feel like a burden. My mother treated him with the utmost respect, always ensuring he felt valued and welcome in our home. Even though my father, a general practitioner, was not earning much at that time, and with mounting expenses for my brother and me as we prepared for medical college, my father sacrificed so much to ensure that we had what we needed.

Though our family faced financial hardships, my father managed to scrape together enough money to purchase a modest one-bedroom apartment in Bhayandar, an up-and-coming suburb in Mumbai, for my uncle. We were living in a small two-bedroom flat in Swaraj Housing Cooperative Society in Vile Parle at the time. Since my uncle was starting his own family, there was simply no room for all of us to live together in the cramped apartment. To resolve this, my father bought the apartment in Bhayandar under his own name but allowed my uncle to reside there as a gesture of goodwill. The sacrifices my family made during those years still resonate with me, especially as I reflect on how I had to forgo certain material comforts at such a young age so that my father could provide for my uncle.

Lingering Resentment

Today, as I look back with a sense of growing resentment, I cannot help but feel anger toward my uncle's attitude. Despite everything my father did for him, he now enjoys his retirement in the United States with his two sons, who have both made a successful living for themselves. Meanwhile, I am still burdened with outstanding loans. My uncle receives a pension from the US government amounting to approximately Rs. 40,000/- every month. *Does he not feel any sense of guilt or responsibility? Even at the age of 90, he continues to cling to the flat that was meant as a temporary gift, a symbol of my father's kindness.*

In the coming chapters, I will delve deeper into how greed transformed a man who should have felt indebted to my father, not only for the support he received but also for the opportunities he was given. Along with my manipulative brother Dolion, they devised a scheme that ultimately resulted in their financial gain at my expense, exposing the darker side of familial relationships.

Childhood Memories

Returning to the story of Roshni, I cannot help but think of the memories we shared as children. I still vividly recall the image of two young girls sitting together on a small bench in the classroom—Kamal and Roshni. *"These are your friends,"* my uncle had said, and from that moment on, our friendship blossomed. It is truly remarkable how friendships formed in childhood can endure the test of time. Even after years of no contact, the bond remains unbroken, woven like an unshakable thread through the fabric of our lives. *True friendship, as I have learned, transcends time and distance. It is a bond that holds steady, offering unwavering support through life's trials and tribulations.*

Gratitude for True Friends

In my previous book, **"When He Held My Hand"**, I expressed my heartfelt gratitude toward my school friends, who stood by me when I was at my lowest. During those challenging times, when I seemed to have no strength left, it was their constant presence and support that helped keep me afloat. Despite my outward appearance of strength, I must admit that without their encouragement, I might have sunk into despair. Of course, I believe it was the Supreme Power who guided me through the darkest times, but it was also these rare, true friends—my gems—who played an integral role in my journey towards healing and resilience. *Today, as I stand where I am, I owe much of my success not only to my own efforts but also to the steadfast support of those dear friends who have remained my pillars of strength.*

Chapter 38

The Unseen Strength of Roshni

A Silent Victim of Gender Discrimination

Roshni, like countless women across the world, especially in India, was a silent victim of gender discrimination. Born into a middle-class family, she grew up under the watchful eyes of strict parents. I still vividly remember our school days together. Roshni was an exceptional student, always at the top of her class, consistently earning stellar grades. After completing her schooling, she pursued a degree in B.Pharm, a field that, in those days, promised lucrative job opportunities with multinational pharmaceutical companies.

Sacrificing Ambitions for Family

However, her journey was far from smooth. Despite her potential and capabilities, her strict parents steered her toward a modest job that aligned with their conservative outlook. These multinational companies often required employees to work flexible hours or travel, demands that her mother deemed unacceptable. To keep her family happy, Roshni dutifully followed their wishes, burying her own ambitions and accepting a life of limited expectations.

Motherhood and Patriarchal Challenges

Eventually, she got married, and soon after, the joys and challenges of motherhood followed. She was blessed with a beautiful daughter. They say *daughters are angels in disguise,* but for Roshni's husband, this blessing was overshadowed by disappointment. He believed a male child would secure their future, while a daughter, in his eyes, would one day leave to start her own family. This patriarchal mindset shaped his actions, and he refused to invest in their daughter's education or even her marriage.

A Mother's Unyielding Determination

But Roshni didn't let this stop her. With quiet determination, she took it upon herself to ensure her daughter received the education she deserved. Every rupee she earned went towards securing her daughter's future, including her wedding expenses. Despite her sacrifices, Roshni's struggles didn't end with her daughter's marriage.

Living Under a Narcissist's Shadow

Her husband's narcissistic tendencies continued to cast a shadow over her life. He imposed his opinions, dictating how she should live and whom she could interact with. Roshni had no freedom to maintain friendships or pursue her own interests. In his eyes, he was the "lord and master," doing her a favor simply by staying in her life. Her existence revolved around pleasing him, often at the cost of her own happiness.

Rejection from Family

When her parents passed away, her brother inherited their family home. Over the years, his health deteriorated, and Roshni would frequently leave her marital home to care for him. Yet, her brother, instead of showing gratitude, accused her of being interested only in the family property. He criticized her for being on her phone, implying that her care was merely for appearances. Back home, her husband would throw tantrums over her absence, adding to her emotional burden.

The Weight of Rejection

Roshni found herself caught in a painful paradox. Despite her tireless dedication to her family, she was met with rejection from both her husband and brother. The weight of these relationships left her feeling unappreciated and dejected.

The Meaning of Rejection

But here's the thing about rejection—it doesn't define your worth. It doesn't mean you're not good enough; it simply reflects others' inability to see your value. Roshni's story resonates with many, especially women who bear the weight of societal and familial expectations without recognition.

Lessons from Adversity

Gautama Buddha once taught that life is a blend of suffering and happiness. Hard times may pin us down, but they are not eternal. What matters is how we respond to these challenges. *Obstacles, when faced with courage, can transform into opportunities, and problems can lead to possibilities.*

Roshni's Resilience

Roshni's story is a testament to resilience. Pain in life is inevitable, but suffering is not. Pain is the reality imposed by the world; suffering is how we internalize that pain. As Buddha wisely said, *"Pain is inevitable, but suffering is optional."* Roshni, in her quiet strength, shows us the bravery of struggling against adversity and the power of hope amidst rejection.

A Universal Reminder

Her journey reminds us all to *find the courage to rise above circumstances, turn obstacles into stepping stones, and embrace life with unyielding determination.*

Chapter 39

A House, a Heist, and a Heartbreaking Injustice

A Brother's Stroke and a Family in Crisis

A few months ago, Roshni was forced to admit her brother to the hospital after he suffered a paralytic stroke. As the ambulance sped away from their old bungalow, a group of beggars stationed at the nearby signal watched intently. The bungalow, though in a dilapidated state, was in a prime location. This made it the target of many opportunists, including street urchins and local builders.

Roshni and her brother had received countless threatening calls over the years. Her brother had repeatedly turned down lucrative offers from builders who wanted to redevelop the property. Despite his declining health and advancing age, he clung to the comfort and familiarity of their ancestral home. Roshni also had a stake in the property, and her husband constantly taunted her, accusing her brother of "sitting on the property like a snake" and refusing to give her the rightful share. Caught between her husband and her brother, Roshni was torn, her loyalties stretched to the breaking point.

Mumbai's Syndicate of Beggars

Roshni had often observed the beggars at the signal near her home. I had seen several movies wherein they show the beggars and their organized operations. It is no secret that in Mumbai, the beggar community often operate under a syndicate system. A kingpin allocates territories, deciding which groups could beg at which signals. Most of their daily earnings are surrendered to the syndicate leader.

I can't comment on the beggars anywhere else in the world, but I know for sure that Mumbai's beggars, are surprisingly wealthy. I had read some time ago, an article in the newspaper, about a beggar who died had savings of ₹50 lakhs and multiple flats across the city.

Mumbai is a city of kind hearted people. At signals, one can see the rich rolling down their windows of their luxury cars, like Mercedes, BMW, Jaguar etc., to hand out wads of cash to beggars posing as crippled or blind individuals. Some even go to the extent of undergoing a limb amputation to get mercy of the public. Children are also roped in to touch the hearts of the mothers and childless couples. Such is the paradox of Mumbai.

A Sinister Heist

The day her brother was hospitalized, Roshni's worst fears came true. As soon as the ambulance left their home, one of the beggars at the signal alerted his accomplices. Within hours, a gang armed with tools broke into the bungalow. They bent and severed the window grills, entered the house, and ransacked it thoroughly.

While there was no jewellery in the house, the gang found copper utensils and other valuable items. Most devastatingly, they discovered currency notes hidden between folds of clothes in various cupboards. Roshni's late mother had painstakingly saved this money, squirreling away small amounts for emergencies. Her brother had followed suit, stashing away his own modest savings. By the end of the heist, the gang had looted approximately ₹5 lakhs—an amount that held immense emotional and financial significance for the middle-class family.

Discovering the Robbery

Two days after her brother was admitted to the hospital, Roshni and her husband visited the bungalow to check on the property. As they approached the bungalow, the beggars at the signal intercepted them, engaging Roshni in conversation to delay her. One of them stepped aside to make a phone call, likely alerting the robbers.

When Roshni reached her home, she saw two men escaping through the bent window grill. The scene inside was devastating—papers strewn across the floor, furniture overturned, and cupboards emptied. The hard-earned money saved by her family was gone. This money meant a lot to her since it held memories of her childhood, seeing her mother saving every penny in order to give a brighter future to her children. For a moment, Roshni thought she might be having a heart attack. Gathering herself, she rushed to the local police station to lodge a complaint.

A Broken System

At the police station, Roshni provided all the details she could. The officers assured her the case would proceed to court. However, Roshni soon learned how difficult it is for someone without money or influence to seek justice.

Three months later, when the case came up in court, *the opposing lawyer made an absurd demand: Roshni had to provide the serial numbers of the currency notes that were missing.* Roshni was aghast. The money in the cupboards was not withdrawn from the bank. The money had been saved gradually—often in small denominations tucked away over the years. The lawyer argued that without proof of the stolen money, and since no jewellery was missing, the case should be dismissed.

The judge, showing little empathy, banged his gavel and declared the case closed. Adding insult to injury, Roshni noticed on the courtroom's display board that her case was registered against a Nepali individual. When she pointed out to the police that none of the beggars she had seen were Nepali, she was dismissed with indifference. Her request to see the accused was met with hostility.

The Cost of Justice

Heartbroken and disillusioned, Roshni returned home. The next day, she confronted the group of beggars at the signal, venting her pain and frustration. She accused them of robbing her family of their hard-earned savings, recounting the sacrifices her mother had made to save every penny. She reminded them that while they might have escaped the law, they could not escape Karma.

Roshni's story is a chilling reminder of how justice often remains elusive for ordinary citizens. For a single woman fighting a powerful syndicate, the odds are insurmountable. Yet, even in her despair, Roshni clung to the hope that Karma would eventually balance the scales.

Justice: Court or Karma?

This story raises poignant questions about the nature of justice. When the legal system fails those without wealth or influence, is Karma the only solace left? For Roshni, the heartbreak of losing her family's savings was compounded by the realization that the system she turned to for justice was indifferent to her plight.

In the end, Roshni's fight for justice remains unresolved. *Her story echoes the struggles of countless others who find themselves powerless in the face of corruption, bureaucracy, and exploitation.* **Whether justice will ever be served—through the Courts or through Karma – remains to be seen.**

Chapter 40

A Life of Dedication and Routine

My paternal grandfather was a well-known and respected civil lawyer in Surat. He epitomized dedication and discipline, his life revolving almost entirely around his work. As a child, I remember his daily routine vividly, as if it were the rhythm of our family life.

Every day, he left for court at precisely 11:00 a.m. and returned home by 5:00 p.m. His bedtime was always 9:00 p.m. sharp. Mornings began with a cup of tea at 7:00 a.m., and evenings were marked by another cup at 5:30 p.m. Lunch was served at 10:00 a.m., while dinner was a quiet affair at 8:00 p.m. His strict adherence to this routine was as integral to his identity as his legal profession.

A Simple Yet Purposeful Life

Rarely did my grandfather venture beyond nearby towns, with occasional trips to cities like Ahmedabad, and these were strictly for court cases, often accompanied by his trusted assistant. Vacations, as we understand them today, were virtually non-existent. I don't recall him ever taking a holiday with my grandmother. This simplicity and focus on duty seemed typical of his time—a life shaped by purpose and obligation.

Despite his unwavering dedication, my grandfather was a man of principle. *His honesty and sincerity earned him an offer to become a judge, but he declined.* The reason was simple yet profound: *becoming a judge meant accepting a mandatory retirement age, and he wanted to work until his last breath.* His love for the law and belief in hard work defined him. Remarkably, he never took a single tablet in his life and remained free of illnesses, passing away peacefully of old age—a life lived with integrity and without regret.

The Quiet Strength of My Grandmother

In contrast, my grandmother was the quiet force behind the family—a devoted homemaker who dedicated her life to cooking and caring for everyone. Together, they had two sons and three daughters. Tragically, two of their daughters passed away shortly after marriage. One succumbed to a grave illness, while the other ended her own life, driven to despair by relentless harassment from her mother-in-law.

This cycle of cruelty was a bitter reality of those times. Mothers-in-law, perhaps carrying forward the pain they had once endured, often tormented their daughters-in-law. This harsh reality was not unique to my aunts; my own mother endured similar struggles after her marriage.

A Life of Quiet Endurance

My mother's life became a series of hardships. She faced torment from her mother-in-law, her husband, and later even from her son and daughter-in-law. Reflecting on her life fills me with sadness. She endured so much, yet never rebelled against the harshness of her circumstances. *Like many Indian women, she accepted suffering as her destiny, a notion deeply ingrained by societal norms.*

But is it truly destiny, or do we have the power to shape our lives? The words of the Supreme Power resonate deeply: **"I have left some pages of your life book blank, my child, for you to write."** While some parts of our fate may be predestined, much of it is ours to create. Unfortunately, many women, including my mother, have lived lives bound by societal expectations, sacrificing their dreams and desires for others.

Gender Bias and Cultural Norms

It's heartbreaking to witness the deeply rooted gender biases in our culture. Even mothers, despite being women themselves, often prioritize their sons over their daughters. Sons are seen as the caretakers of parents in old age, yet it is often daughters who step up to care for their aging parents. Sons, meanwhile, frequently drift away after marriage, caught up in their own lives.

This preference for male children is fueled by the desire to continue the family legacy, often overlooking the immense emotional and practical support daughters provide. **Will this gender disparity ever end?** It's a haunting question. Perhaps the solution lies in reevaluating our values and dismantling these entrenched biases.

A Vision for Equality

I often think of Michael Jackson's iconic song, *"Heal the World."* While it speaks of global peace and harmony, for me, it resonates differently. *I dream of a world healed of gender discrimination, where justice is swift and impartial, and everyone receives fair treatment under the law.*

Justice delayed is justice denied. Too often, cases drag on for decades, leaving victims emotionally and financially drained. By the time justice is served, they are either no longer alive or too broken to find solace in the verdict.

Writing a New Chapter

Let us strive for a world where no one suffers in silence, where women are valued as equals, and where justice is not a luxury but a right. *Together, we can write a new chapter on those blank pages—one of hope, equality, and compassion.*

Chapter 41

The Legacy of My Grandfather

Coming to the story of my grandfather, I am filled with awe and a deep sense of pride for the man he was. His life was a testament to hard work, integrity, and an unwavering commitment to fairness. Despite toiling endlessly well into his old age, he remained unassuming in his lifestyle, choosing simplicity over extravagance. Yet, his diligence and frugality allowed him to amass considerable wealth, both material and moral.

My grandfather was an exceptional civil lawyer, revered for his honesty and fairness. What made him stand out, even more, was his progressive mind-set—remarkably rare in those times. *He treated his sons and daughters equally, an ideology almost unheard of in an era when daughters were often considered second to sons.* He set up three separate bank accounts for his two sons and one daughter, ensuring financial equality among them. His other two daughters had passed away long before, leaving me with no memories of them.

One vivid memory I hold is of my cousin, who often assisted my grandfather with his bank work. My grandfather would hand him equal amounts of cash to deposit in the three accounts. This act of fairness and impartiality inspires me to this day. *How incredible it is to think that while modern society struggles with such values, my grandfather lived them effortlessly decades ago.*

His investments in shares were another testament to his acumen. My cousin recounts how my grandfather would receive wads of dividends from multinational companies weekly, which he diligently deposited in the bank. Today, the market value of those shares is an astounding ₹5 crores. Tragically, all of it has been swallowed up by my brother, Dolion. ***How he manages to look at himself in the mirror every day is beyond me!*** *Does it never occur to him that the shares rightfully belong to all nine grandchildren?* My father has two children, my paternal uncle has three, and my paternal aunt has four. ***Yet Dolion, like a lion consuming its prey, has selfishly claimed the shares meant for eight other people.***

A Test of Integrity

Fairness was not just a principle for my grandfather, it was his way of life. His brilliant legal mind could have made him an exceptional judge, carving his name in history as a man who dispensed justice without fear or favour. One incident, etched deeply in my mind, perfectly illustrates his unwavering commitment to justice.

One day, he handed a significant amount of money to my paternal uncle, instructing him to deposit it equally into the three accounts. However, my uncle, driven by jealousy and greed, deposited the entire sum into his own account, believing no one would ever find out. When my grandfather discovered the betrayal, he was livid. A man who lived and breathed fairness could not tolerate such deceit, especially from his own son.

He immediately ordered my uncle to leave his home and scolded my grandmother for failing to instil better values in their son. Overwhelmed by shame, my uncle left Surat that very day, boarding a train to Bombay. Years later, even when his son needed to stay in Surat for college, my uncle couldn't muster the courage to approach my grandfather. As a result, his son spent three years in a hostel, while my grandfather, unwavering in his principles, refused to offer his bungalow as accommodation.

Building a Legacy

My grandfather's practice was unique in its inclusivity—he charged nominal fees and catered to both the wealthy and the poor. Once, a client, unable to pay in cash, offered him a plot of land as payment. Another client, an architect, designed and constructed my grandfather's bungalow as compensation for legal services. My grandmother played an instrumental role in this process. Every day, she would oversee the construction site, managing bricks and cement deliveries with the meticulousness of a contractor.

This bungalow, built through the sweat and toil of my grandparents, was later usurped and sold by Dolion, who falsely claimed it as his own. My grandfather's will had clearly stated that the bungalow was to be shared between his two sons after my aunt relinquished her rights. Yet the betrayal of this legacy by my own family remains a deep wound.

A Mother's Sacrifice

After my grandmother's death, my grandfather chose to stay alone in Surat, his life centered entirely around his work. When my father suggested that my uncle's wife move to Surat to care for him, she refused outright. My father, enraged by her indifference, compelled my mother to take up the responsibility. A meek and mild woman, my mother dutifully packed her bags and shifted to Surat.

Back in Bombay, I took over the household responsibilities. Each morning, I prepared tea, breakfast, and packed tiffins for my father, brother, and myself. I cooked, cleaned, and managed the home, balancing these duties with my studies. ***Looking back, I can't help but wonder—has Dolion forgotten the countless meals I prepared for him?***

The saying **"a snake bites the hand that feeds it"** has never felt more apt.

The End of an Era

Eventually, my grandfather's health declined, forcing him to move to Mumbai. For me, this marked the end of my household responsibilities, allowing me to focus solely on my education. After his passing, my father displayed a surprising level of animosity towards his brother. He coerced my uncle into relinquishing his rights to the Surat bungalow, making my father its sole owner.

Yet, my father seemed oblivious to the concept of Karma. His last decade was marred by suffering, orchestrated by none other than his son and daughter-in-law, Dolion and Batibat. Even his death was surrounded by a web of deceit, culminating in a forged will prepared by Dolion. This fraudulent document claimed that I had relinquished all my rights to our family's properties and assets, an act I would never have consented to.

Betrayal and Legacy

Dolion's greed knew no bounds. He went so far as to file an affidavit declaring himself the sole child of my parents, erasing me entirely from the narrative. ***It's painful to see the legacy of a man as noble as my grandfather tarnished by the selfish actions of his descendants.***

As I reflect on these events, I find solace in the belief that Karma spares no one. My grandfather's life was a beacon of fairness and integrity, and while it's disheartening to witness how far some have strayed, his values remain a guiding light for those of us who choose to honour his memory.

An Appeal

I appeal to the Universe that let wisdom prevail on Dolion and Batibat and make them rectify their misdeeds. They must be reminded that Karma is a slow, moving bus but it does not skip any stops.

Making peace

Coming to peace with past mistakes can be a challenging but transformative process. Here are some steps you can take to help you find that peace:

1) *Acknowledge Your Mistakes*:

   Recognize and accept what you've done. Reflect on the situation and understand the choices you made.

2) *Understand the Context*:

   Consider the circumstances that led to your decisions. Often, mistakes are made under pressure or lack of information. Understanding the context can help you be kinder to yourself.

3) *Learn from the Experience*:

   Identify the lessons you can take away from your mistakes. What would you do differently now? This reflection can turn a negative experience into a valuable learning opportunity.

4) *Practice Self-Compassion:*

Treat yourself with the same kindness and understanding you would offer a friend. Remind yourself that everyone makes mistakes and that you are not defined by them.

5) *Apologize if Necessary:*

If your mistakes have hurt others, consider reaching out to apologize or make amends. This can help heal relationships and give you a sense of closure.

6) *Focus on the Present:*

Shift your attention to the present moment. Engage in activities that bring you joy and fulfilment. Mindfulness practices can be particularly helpful in keeping you grounded.

7) *Seek Support:*

Talk to friends, family, or a mental health professional about your feelings. Sometimes, sharing your thoughts can help you process them more effectively.

8) *Forgive Yourself:*

Ultimately, forgiveness is a key step. Recognize that you are human and that making mistakes is part of life. Let go of the guilt and allow yourself to move forward.

9) *Set New Goals:*

Redirect your energy towards positive goals and aspirations. Focus on what you want to achieve moving forward rather than dwelling on the past.

10) *Reflect Regularly*:

Make it a habit to reflect on your thoughts and feelings about your past. Journaling can be a helpful tool for this, as it allows you to express and process your emotions.

Finding peace with past mistakes is a journey that takes time and effort. Be patient with yourself as you work through these feelings.

Chapter 42

A Life-Changing Decision

As mentioned in earlier chapters, my father once made a life-changing decision for his financially struggling brother, my paternal uncle. Years ago, my uncle lived with us for a long time, and when he eventually started his own family, my father took it upon himself to arrange a rental apartment for him. Not only did he cover the rent, but he also extended financial support to help my uncle manage his household. My ever-generous mother, who shared my father's sense of duty and compassion, ensured that their monthly groceries were taken care of as well. It was her way of expressing love and care, embodying the spirit of family support.

Purchasing a Home for My Uncle

After years of saving, my father purchased a modest one-bedroom apartment for my uncle in the Mit Milan Cooperative Housing Society in Bhayandar. This act of generosity defined my parents—selfless, supportive, and always putting family first. They continued to support my uncle's household until his children became independent.

My cousins, intelligent and hardworking, earned scholarships to study in Germany and eventually settled in the United States with lucrative careers. Their sister married into a wealthy family and now resides in Thane, Mumbai.

The Present Situation: A Neglected Property

Fast forward to today: my uncle, now 90 years old, enjoys a comfortable life with a generous U.S. government pension of ₹40,000 per month. Yet, the Bhayandar apartment, purchased by my father, has been locked and neglected for over a decade. The property has fallen into disrepair, but my uncle stubbornly refuses to hand over the keys or relinquish control.

This situation has only added to my frustrations, as I strongly suspect the involvement of Dolion—a manipulative and narcissistic individual who has already taken over my parents' two flats in Swaraj Housing Cooperative Society, in Vile Parle. Dolion's vendetta against me seems to be fuelled by my ongoing court battles with him in Mumbai and Surat, where I have become his prime target.

Questionable Transactions and Legal Battles

Dolion's influence over my uncle appears evident, as the flat's paperwork has allegedly been tampered with to create hurdles for me. Despite the challenges, I remain determined to fight. Just months before his passing, my father urged me to claim what was rightfully mine. He knew about the financial burdens I was carrying as a single mother managing multiple EMIs. Although he felt powerless against Dolion and Batibat, he blessed me with the courage to stand firm and fight for justice.

My lawyer has sent multiple letters to the Mit Milan Cooperative Housing Society, but their office bearers have remained unresponsive. Despite receiving four notices from the registrar, the society has failed to provide any documentation related to the flat. The nameplate on the flat still bears my uncle's name, but my father had confided in me that he never gifted the flat to his brother or signed any documents transferring ownership. This raises a troubling question: ***how did the flat my father purchased end up being associated with my uncle?***

Suspicious Deeds and Family Manipulations

In March 2024, my 90-year-old uncle travelled to India for his granddaughter's wedding. I was not invited, thanks to Dolion's influence. During this visit, my uncle executed a gift deed transferring 100% ownership of the Bhayandar flat to his son. Astonishingly, the very next day, his son executed another gift deed, transferring 50% of his share to his wife. ***Two gift deeds on consecutive days—the entire sequence reeks of foul play.***

The glaring issue here is that my uncle has no legitimate paperwork to prove how the flat was transferred from my father's name to his own. If the flat isn't even legally in his name, how could he gift it to his son? And how could his son, in turn, transfer half of it to his wife? Where are the society's approvals or the documents validating these transactions? This situation screams of a serious criminal offense, and my case with the registrar is focused on exposing these irregularities.

Fighting for Justice

Last month, in November 2024, my uncle's lawyer submitted papers in court. These documents have only deepened the mystery and strengthened my resolve. ***My father's hard-earned money cannot be allowed to benefit people who have ignored me for over 25 years.*** The nephew in question is someone I last saw when he was in college, and his wife is a complete stranger to me.

I have filed this case under Section 154-B9 with the Bhayandar Registrar of Societies and am awaiting the results with cautious optimism. *My father's legacy and sacrifices deserve justice, and I will not stop until the truth prevails.*

A Fight Beyond Property

This fight is not just about property; it is about honouring the values my parents stood for and ensuring that their kindness and sacrifices are not exploited by those who don't deserve it.

Chapter 43

Friday the 13ᵗʰ

An Ominous Day of Irony

Friday the 13th—a day steeped in superstition and foreboding. For me, this date bears a cruel twist of fate. It was on this day that I received an order from the registrar in Bandra regarding my late father's flat in Swaraj Cooperative Housing Society.

This flat, initially purchased by my father in his brother's name, had mysteriously been transferred to Dolion without any legal documentation. When I filed a petition under Section 154 B9 (this section was suggested by the previous registrar) to investigate this glaring irregularity, the present registrar dismissed it, claiming that too many years had elapsed for any action to be taken.

A System That Fails the Honest

What kind of justice is this? I unearthed this troubling truth only after my father's passing in 2020. During his lifetime, I had never questioned him about property matters—it felt improper for a child to demand answers about their parents' assets.

But now, faced with blatant deceit, I see the cracks in our system. The registrar's argument was absurd: Dolion, having lived in the flat for years, supposedly had no obligation to present legal documents. *By that logic, anyone could occupy a stranger's home and claim ownership simply by residing there.*

The Stench of Corruption

This order reeks of corruption. Dolion, with his cunning mind and deep pockets, appears to have greased the wheels of bureaucracy. ***Whispers in the corridors suggest he paid ₹25 lakhs to secure this favorable decision.*** The collusion between him and the authorities is palpable.

Family Betrayal and Forged Documents

The plot thickened with my Bhayandar case. My 90-year-old paternal uncle recently produced suspicious documents to bolster his claim to the flat. These papers, undoubtedly forged, seem to be part of Dolion's grand scheme.

His motive is transparent: he aims to secure the ₹7-crore flat in Swaraj Housing Cooperative Society while manipulating my uncle into feeling indebted to him. In return, my uncle stands to gain ill-gotten possession of a ₹3-crore flat in Bhayandar. It's a calculated move—typical of Dolion's shrewd and narcissistic nature.

The Moral Decay Within Families

It's disheartening to see a man as old as my uncle stooping to such levels for wealth. This saga has not only exposed the depths of Dolion's greed but also the moral decay within families. As I grapple with this uphill battle, I am forced to confront the larger issues that plague our society.

Corruption: A Low-Risk, High-Profit Game

The Ubiquity of Corruption

In a nation riddled with poverty and inequality, corruption thrives. Honor and integrity often bow to the lure of material gain. Many people, outwardly pious and moral, secretly master fraud and deception. Money erases sins and silences dissent.

Rarely do individuals—perhaps less than 1%—dare to act honorably in the face of corruption. Those who do often face hostility, as corrupt networks operate like well-oiled machines, protecting their own.

A Chilling Perspective

Once, I heard a junior officer casually justify his habit of taking bribes. When questioned about the risk of losing his job or being arrested, he responded with a chilling analogy:

> *"Do soldiers stop joining the army because they hear about deaths at the border? No. Similarly, corrupt officers don't stop taking bribes because the chances of getting caught are even slimmer than the risks soldiers face."*

His twisted logic reflects an undeniable truth. Corruption persists because it's a low-risk, high-reward venture.

The Need for Systemic Reform

As Mr. N. Vittal, former Chief Vigilance Commissioner of India, aptly stated, *"Corruption flourishes because it is a low-risk, high-profit activity."* The solution lies in raising the stakes.

We need robust anti-corruption mechanisms and greater transparency. Automating processes to reduce human discretion could also help. Until then, individuals like Dolion will continue exploiting the system, leaving behind a trail of injustice.

A Fight Beyond the Personal

As I stand at this crossroads on a day as ominous as Friday the 13th, I remind myself that this battle is not just about reclaiming what is mine. *It's a fight against corruption, greed, and deceit—a fight for a fairer, more just world.*

Friday the 13th, a day often associated with misfortune, seems almost poetic in its alignment with my current plight. But unlike superstitions, my battle is rooted in cold, harsh realities. I am left questioning not only the fairness of our system but also the meaning of honor, family, and justice in a world where even the most sacred bonds can be tainted by greed.

Chapter 44

The Tragic Tale of Judas Iscariot:

Consequences of Betrayal

Judas Iscariot's story is one of the most haunting accounts in history, a narrative that transcends religious boundaries to serve as a timeless cautionary tale. His betrayal of Jesus Christ, an act driven by greed and perhaps disillusionment, led to a series of events that underline the weight of moral choices and their irreversible consequences.

Remorse: The Burden of Guilt

After witnessing Jesus condemned to death, Judas was overwhelmed with remorse. He returned the thirty pieces of silver—the price of his betrayal—to the chief priests and elders, confessing, *"I have sinned, for I have betrayed innocent blood."* But his attempt at restitution could not undo his actions. The silver, now deemed ***"blood money,"*** could not absolve him of his guilt, leaving Judas consumed by despair.

Suicide: A Final Escape

Matthew 27 recounts how Judas, unable to bear the weight of his guilt, took his own life by hanging. His tragic end serves as a stark reminder of how unchecked greed and betrayal can lead to personal ruin, leaving no room for redemption in one's own mind.

The "Field of Blood" and Sudden Death

In the Book of Acts, another account of Judas's demise is recorded. It tells of how he purchased a field with his ill-gotten gains and met a sudden, gruesome death there. The field came to be known as *Akeldama*, or the **"Field of Blood,"** a physical and symbolic testament to the cost of betrayal.

Eternal Condemnation

In Christian tradition, Judas's ultimate punishment is said to extend beyond the physical realm. The Council of Trent affirmed that Judas was condemned to Hell—a spiritual consequence that underscores the gravity of his actions. *His story resonates as a warning about the perils of disloyalty and the eternal ramifications of our choices.*

The Legacy of Judas and the Number 13

Judas's betrayal also ties into the symbolism of Friday the 13th. In Christianity, Judas was the thirteenth guest at the Last Supper, a detail that has contributed to the superstition surrounding the number 13. Similarly, in Norse mythology, the uninvited trickster god Loki disrupted a feast of 12 gods, leading to chaos and death. In both traditions, the number 13 represents misfortune and betrayal.

Lessons for Modern Times:

A Reflection on Dolion

The tale of Judas continues to echo in the modern world, where greed and deceit often take center stage. Take Dolion, for instance—a man who believes bribery ensures success. While his corrupt ways may yield results 90% of the time, the remaining 10% holds the potential for devastating consequences. **All it takes is one honest soul to expose his actions, leaving Dolion's life in ruins.**

What drives such behavior? Like Judas, it may be greed, a sense of entitlement, or a disregard for morality. But history, myth, and even personal experiences teach us that the consequences of such actions are unavoidable. *Betrayal and deceit ultimately lead to isolation, regret, and destruction—whether in life, reputation, or legacy.*

Conclusion:

The Weight of Choices

Judas Iscariot's life is a powerful reminder of the moral and spiritual consequences of our decisions. His story implores us to examine our own lives, weigh our actions carefully, and choose integrity over short-term gains. ***Betrayal may promise momentary success, but as Judas's life shows, the cost is far too great.***

Chapter 45

Reflections on the Pursuit of Justice

Sacrifices on the Path to Truth

As I sit back and reflect, I realize the pursuit of justice has come at a heavy cost—sacrificing many relationships along the way. These sacrifices weren't by choice but by revelation. One by one, people revealed their true colours, and the journey toward truth became lonelier with each passing day. What began as a collective fight for righteousness has dwindled into an individual battle, filled with self-discovery and resilience.

The Initial Support and Its Disappearance

When I first began this fight for justice, the support was overwhelming. Well-wishers enthusiastically pledged their allegiance, vowing to stand with me until the very end. Their words were filled with promises of unwavering loyalty, and their presence gave me a sense of strength and hope. Yet, as time passed, the façade faded, and reality revealed itself. Their enthusiasm was fleeting, and their promises shallow.

Life feels like a train journey with a predetermined destination. Initially, the train was packed with people I held dear, some for decades, others for over half a century. I had selflessly supported them—providing medical aid, running errands, or simply being their pillar. Many even joined hands with me in this battle because they too had grievances against Dolion and Batibat. However, some merely sought to use me, putting the gun on my shoulder to fire their shots. Their selfish motives became apparent only when the stakes grew higher, and their commitment wavered.

Dolion's Schemes and My Resolve

In this age of Kalyug, power and money speak louder than words. Dolion, a covert narcissist, knew this well. His goal was singular—to isolate me, thinking I would crumble under the weight of loneliness. *Ever since I returned to my parents' home (a move I have written about in my previous book, **"When He Held My Hand"**), his scheming began in earnest. To him, I was a thorn in his grand plan to usurp what belonged to my family and ancestors.*

- Dolion underestimated me, trapped in his archaic belief that women are neither entitled to ancestral rights nor possess the strength to challenge the status quo. He ignored the **Hindu Succession Act of 2005, which clearly states that daughters and sons have equal**

rights to their parents' and ancestors' assets. His malevolence grew when he realized I was no pawn in his game. Every move I made countered his, exposing his web of deceit. My resilience and determination to fight back became the greatest threat to his schemes.

Gaslighting and the Departure of Fair-weather Friends

Dolion used Gaslighting as his weapon of choice, employing his "flying monkeys" to carry out his bidding. Slowly, station by station, he orchestrated their departure from my train, luring them with promises and manipulation. By 2024, my train had grown lighter. Most of the passengers who lacked integrity or carried negative energy had disembarked. While their absence stung, it was also liberating. My train, now lighter, moves faster. The few who remain are pure in spirit, loyal, and aligned with my dreams. Their unwavering support and kindness have become the fuel that keeps me moving forward.

Lessons from Betrayals

As I reflect on the betrayals and shifting alliances, I've come to realize something profound: a person's true nature is revealed in their moments of vulnerability. Masks slip, pretences fade, and authenticity surfaces. Over the years, I've observed several scenarios that unveil one's character. Here's what I've learned, corroborated by insights from mental health professionals:

1) *In Adversity:*

True colours emerge during tough times. It's easy to be kind when life is smooth, but challenges test the depth of someone's compassion and resilience. Watch how people behave when the storm hits. Some rise with grace, while others falter, revealing their selfish nature.

2)   *In Positions of Power:*

Power magnifies true character. Some grow humble and wise, while others become arrogant and dismissive. Authority exposes whether someone is a leader or a tyrant. It's in these moments that one's values and principles shine through.

3)   *When Facing Tough Choices:*

Dilemmas reveal values. Whether someone chooses honesty over deceit or loyalty over betrayal speaks volumes about their core beliefs. Actions taken during these times often leave a lasting impact, defining a person's legacy.

4)   *When No One Is Watching:*

A person's true integrity lies in what they do when there's no audience. Do they remain honest, or do they take shortcuts when they think no one will notice? This silent measure of character speaks louder than any public display of virtue.

5)   *Under Family Pressure:*

Family ties can sometimes overshadow friendships. It's disheartening but true—some people alter their loyalties when influenced by their spouse, children, or relatives. This shifting allegiance often reveals their priorities and the fragility of their commitments.

6) *When Asked for Help:*

Willingness to help without expecting anything in return is a hallmark of genuine kindness. Observe whether someone extends a hand only when it serves their interests. True friends and allies give selflessly, without calculating the benefits.

7) *During Moments of Crisis:*

Crises strip away the masks we wear. How someone reacts under pressure—whether with grace or selfishness—reveals their true self. It is in these moments that one's humanity is tested, for better or worse.

Moving Forward with Strength and Clarity

Carl Jung once said, *"You are what you do, not what you say you'll do."* Actions, particularly during challenging times, speak louder than any words ever can. Over time, I've learned that in Kalyug, power and material wealth draw crowds. Values like honesty, righteousness, and integrity often go unnoticed, even mocked. Yet, I hold onto a simple truth: *"When someone truly cares about you, they make an effort, not an excuse."* Effort, no matter how small, always trumps empty words.

As 2024 ends and 2025 begins, I find solace in the realization that everything happens for a reason. My train now carries only those with positive energy. The betrayals, though painful, were blessings in disguise, clearing my path and lightening my load. I have learned to stand strong alone, to find peace in solitude, and to trust in the Justice of Karma. Each departure, each betrayal, has been a step toward a purer journey, free of negativity and filled with authentic connections.

I know this journey is far from over, but I am certain of one thing: it will all be worth it in the end. As I march forward, I take with me a painful lesson.

I know that in the end, I will remember not the words of my enemies, but the silence of my well-wishers who betrayed me.

Justice may be delayed, but it will never be denied. This truth gives me the courage to press on, knowing that Karma never forgets and that integrity will always trump in the end.

Chapter 46

Conclusions Drawn

As the calendar turns to January 2025, I find myself looking back and reflecting on a journey that has spanned three long and challenging years. These years have been marked by an incessant pursuit of justice, as I have fought tirelessly for my legal rights. Despite the countless hours spent in preparation, the multiple appearances in court, and the ongoing battle against bureaucracy, concrete results on the legal front remain elusive. I continue to navigate an intricate maze of paperwork, meetings, and decisions, always moving from one obstacle to the next, without a clear resolution in sight. It often feels like a relentless cycle that demands more patience and perseverance than I had ever imagined. However, there is an old saying that has given me strength: ***the effort itself is a measure of success, not just the final outcome***. In this regard, I consider myself successful, not because of what has been achieved externally, but because of the internal fortitude I have built through this experience.

Navigating Disappointments

Every appearance in the court of law has been a test of resilience, often culminating in disappointment or frustration. Each day spent in legal proceedings has added another layer of challenge to an already difficult journey. Yet, despite the setbacks, I have developed a personal practice that has helped me navigate these challenges with grace and persistence. This practice involves four crucial steps, or tests, that I go through each time I face adversity:

1) *Acceptance*:

   I make peace with what has happened, no matter how discouraging or unfair it might seem. I tell myself, "It's fine," accepting that things haven't gone as planned and that I must move forward from here.

2) *Positive Perspective*:

   I strive to embrace the belief that whatever has transpired, however difficult it may be, has happened for my own good. There is a hidden lesson in every challenge, and I try to see the silver lining, even when it seems elusive.

3) *Self-Reflection*:

   I take a moment to pause and ask myself if I have genuinely given my all in this process. Have I put in 100% of my effort? Have I made any mistakes or missed opportunities that I could learn from? This reflection helps me grow and evolve as a person, regardless of the outcome.

4) *Renewed Determination:*

Lastly, I remind myself of my goal and the larger purpose that drives me. I resolve to try again, to start fresh with renewed determination, and to give it my best once more.

With each setback, I reaffirm my commitment to giving my all. I persist with unwavering determination, even when it feels like the world is conspiring against me. Despite Dolion's attempts to break me financially, mentally, and emotionally, I remain steadfast and strong, unwilling to let go of my integrity and resolve.

Spiritual Growth

Amidst the turbulence and chaos of these three long years, something profound has taken place within me. A transformation, one that I never anticipated but now deeply value, has occurred. I have become more spiritually inclined and introspective, gaining valuable insights into the nature of life, the human experience, and the workings of the Universe.

I have come to understand, at a deeper level, ***that the Universe is teaching me patience in all aspects of my life. This lesson of patience is not just about waiting for outcomes, but about finding peace within myself, accepting the process, and trusting that all things unfold in their own time.*** I am grateful for this lesson, as difficult as it has been, for it has shaped me into someone who can now face adversity with greater strength and understanding.

Embracing Life's Journey

Through this journey, I have come to realize that life is not a destination, but a process—a journey composed of many different parts, twists, and turns. Each path I choose, whether it leads to triumph or failure, becomes part of my destiny, contributing to the person I am becoming.

With this understanding in mind, I offer a sincere prayer to the Supreme Power:

"If I ever find myself on the verge of losing hope, or if I feel that my purpose is slipping away, may I be granted the confidence to trust that my destiny is unfolding exactly as it should. May I remember that the path ahead is more beautiful and meaningful than anything I could have ever imagined, even when the road is rough and uncertain".

In conclusion, while the battles continue and the challenges persist, I hold on to the belief that success is not simply about the outcomes, but about the growth, resilience, and strength gained along the way. Every step, every struggle, and every failure has contributed to making me the person I am today. I am committed to this journey, no matter how long it takes, and I am ready to embrace whatever comes next with faith, resilience, and a renewed sense of purpose. The path ahead may still be unclear, but I walk it with the certainty that I will continue to evolve and learn, becoming ever stronger and wiser with each passing day.

Epilogue

Do Karma and Justice Exist in Today's World?

"It takes a long time to learn that a courtroom is the last place in our world for learning the truth."
— Alice Koller

The idea of justice has captivated human consciousness for centuries. Yet, the real world often presents a far less idealistic picture. Rarely do we find the clarity and resolution depicted in courtroom dramas.

As crime analyst Pat Brown aptly put it, *"In reality, those rare few cases with substantial forensic evidence are the ones that make it to court."*

The courtroom, which many view as a bastion of truth and justice, can often feel like a stage for bureaucracy, posturing, and delayed verdicts.

Disillusionment and Reality

One young woman, inspired by her father's thrilling tales of the courtroom, embarked on a legal battle with great expectations. She imagined intense debates, the pursuit of truth, and the triumph of justice. But the reality was starkly different. Instead of fiery arguments and ground-breaking revelations, she found herself buried under piles of paperwork and procedural details. The system she once revered seemed distant from the justice she envisioned.

This disillusionment is not unique. Many grapple with the question: does justice truly prevail in today's world? Or has it become a shadow of its ideal form, tangled in a web of inefficiency and human frailty?

Justice and the Lens of Karma

Justice, in its truest form, aligns with the Universal Principle of Karma—the idea that every action has consequences. Hindu philosophy eloquently states, *"A judge who declares the wicked innocent will be cursed by many, and denounced by nations. But those who convict the guilty will receive blessings."* This resonates deeply with the essence of Karma, a concept that transcends spiritual beliefs and offers a framework for understanding cause and effect in human behaviour.

Demystifying Karma

Karma is often misunderstood as mere fate or destiny. But in essence, it's a profound and logical science governed by three key principles:

1) *Action and Its Effect:*

Every deed sets in motion a chain of consequences.

2) *Impressions on the Mind:*

Actions leave subtle marks on our psyche, shaping our habits and tendencies.

3) *Action Driven by Impressions:*

These mental imprints influence our future actions, creating patterns that define our lives.

For example, consider the habit of morning coffee. Over time, this simple ritual becomes ingrained. The day coffee is unavailable, discomfort arises—not because coffee is inherently essential, but because the mind has been conditioned to expect it. This repetitive cycle is what we might call "coffee karma."

The Science of Karma

Karma mirrors Newton's third law: every action has an equal and opposite reaction. If someone steals, and ends up in prison, their action of stealing resulted in the Karma of being incarcerated. Similarly, it was the police officer's Karma to catch the thief.

Karma is a chain reaction. Even inaction brings Karma. A judge who refuses to hear a case or delays a verdict accumulates Karma for his neglect.

The ripple effects of Karma are infinite and intricate, prompting Hindu scriptures to describe it as **"Gahana Karma No Gathi"** —*mysterious and unfathomable.*

The Enigma of Timing

When will Karma manifest? This is one of life's great mysteries. Some Karmic seeds sprout quickly, like a tomato plant, while others, like a mango tree, take years—or even lifetimes. This unpredictability often leads to frustration and doubt about the fairness of life, but the truth lies in patience and perspective.

Embracing Karma in Daily Life

How, then, should one live in harmony with Karma? The answer is simple yet profound: **surrender**. By relinquishing attachment to outcomes and focusing on the purity of our actions, we break free from the binding chains of Karma.

Practices like meditation and yoga help cleanse the mind of residual impressions, creating a state of mental clarity and balance. Living with awareness, doing good, and embracing challenges with a smile transforms the way we perceive life's trials.

A Journey of Grace

Ultimately, Karma and Justice are not abstract concepts but guides for living with integrity and mindfulness. By aligning our actions with kindness and surrendering the results to the greater flow of life, we become co-creators of a just and harmonious world.

So, do Karma and Justice exist? Perhaps the answer lies in how we choose to embody them in our lives. Keep doing good, trust in the process, and let the Universe take care of the rest.

This epilogue serves as a contemplative closure to our exploration of Karma and Justice, offering readers a deeper understanding and personal connection to these timeless concepts.

The Path of Destiny: A Journey of Choice and Divine Guidance

The Power of Destiny

Every soul is said to carry a unique destiny, a map laid out long before birth. The journey, however, requires more than passive acceptance—it demands trust, courage, and the will to walk the path, regardless of its twists and turns. This profound idea finds its expression in a timeless conversation between a child and God.

The child asks earnestly, *"If everything is already written in destiny, why do we need to wish?"* With a knowing smile, God replies, *"Perhaps on some pages, I have written, 'as you wish.'"* This tender exchange reveals a deep truth: Destiny is not a rigid script but a dynamic partnership, a story written both *for us* and *with us*. It suggests that Divine Guidance and human choice together weave the fabric of our lives.

***

The Journey of Life: Fate vs. Destiny

Life is often likened to a journey—a quest where we navigate the terrain between two forces: **fate** and **destiny**.

Fate, in its most challenging form, represents the weight of life's struggles—the heartbreaks, the disappointments, the wounds that threaten to hold us down. It is what happens when we surrender to life's difficulties without resistance.

Destiny, however, is the triumph over these very trials. It is the higher calling, the potential for transformation that lies dormant within each obstacle. When we rise above adversities, when we dare to turn setbacks into stepping stones, destiny reveals itself as an opportunity for growth, self-discovery, and fulfilment. By choosing to embrace destiny, we transcend mere survival and step into the realm of purpose and meaning.

* * *

Taking Control of Your Destiny

To take control of your destiny, you must first believe in yourself. Doubt and fear will always knock at your door, often disguised as the voices of naysayers or the shadows of past failures. But to shape your future, you must silence these distractions and surround yourself with positivity. Seek out uplifting people, environments, and habits that align with your goals.

Perseverance is your greatest ally. The road will not always be easy; challenges may test your resolve. But remember this: greatness is born not of ease but of endurance. Never give in to despair or abandon your dreams.

Too many wander aimlessly through life, drifting without purpose or vision. They allow others to steer their course, handing over the reins of their destiny. Without dreams or a plan to achieve them, life becomes a mere reaction to circumstances—a script written by someone else. To reclaim your story, you must actively engage with your desires, setting clear goals and taking deliberate steps to realize them.

✳ ✳ ✳

Conclusion: A Message of Hope and Faith

The journey of life finds its ultimate anchor in hope and faith. The promise of Divine Justice is beautifully captured in these powerful words from the Bible:

> *"Listen! I am coming soon! I will bring reward with me, and I will repay each one of you for what you have done. I am the Alpha and the Omega, the First and the Last, the Beginning and the End."*

> *— Revelation 22:12-13 NKJV*

This passage reminds us of an eternal truth: we are not alone in our efforts to shape our destinies. Divine Justice walks hand in hand with human will, offering rewards for perseverance, courage, and faith. It assures us that every choice, every act of resilience, contributes to a grander purpose.

In the end, life is not about merely following a path—it's about co-creating it. Trust in your potential, embrace the Divine Plan, and step boldly into the Destiny that awaits you.

– Dr. Crystal

'WHEN HE HELD MY HAND'

This soul-stirring biography, "When He held my hand," is a candid narrative of a woman, depicting her eventful journey from childhood to old age.

Blurb

Various shades of her life have been written, which also includes exposing the harsh realities and shocking truths.

Some of the several thought-provoking topics revealed in this enticing book are gender discrimination, harassment, manipulations, hidden secrets, and even suspense over the attempt to murder!

This engaging book will also enable you to:

- Take charge of your life as you ensure that life happens for you and not to you.

- Become more successful by turning weaknesses into strengths.

- Building more confidence through your positive thought processes.

- Accomplish much more by removing the barriers that prevent you from living a fulfilling life.

While reading this motivational book, you will find how ever-increasing flow of miracles is experienced in life.

As the name rightfully suggests, this book will undoubtedly strengthen your faith in yourself and the Supreme Power.

"And once the storm is over, you will not remember how you made it through, how you managed to survive. You will not even be sure, whether the storm is really over. But one thing is certain. When you come out of the storm, you will not be the same person who walked in. That's what the storm is about." - Haruki Murakami.